How to Use This Kit

Page Numbering

Each page in *Teacher's Activity Kit*, Book 3 is labeled at the top with a Unit number, Activity number, and a correlating page reference.

- The Unit number tells which Unit of *Alfred's Essentials of Music Theory*, Book 3 contains the topic the Activity reinforces.
- The Activity number indicates the sequence of Activities within each Unit.
- The specific page in *Alfred's Essentials of Music Theory*, Book 3 with which the Activity may be assigned is given at the upper right-hand corner of each sheet. When more than one Activity correlates to the same page in the *Essentials of Music Theory* text book, the Activities may be assigned in any order.
- There is also a space at the top of each page for the student to write his or her name and class.

Scorekeeping

Each Activity and Test page indicates how points are to be scored so that the page may be graded. The point system to be used is determined by the type of exercises on the page.

A box divided into halves will appear to the right of each exercise.

- If a box has only one number in the bottom half, it indicates a flat score for that exercise.
- If a box has two numbers in the bottom half, the first number indicates the number of points to score for each individual correct answer within the exercise. The second number indicates the total number of points that can be earned for correctly answering all the items in that exercise.
- The top half of the box is for you to record the number of points actually earned for the exercise.

Every page has a three-part box at the bottom where the scores and total grade for that page are recorded. The total for each page is always 100.

Record Keeping

At the back of the Kit (page 48) is a record keeping form for listing students and all their grades, organized by Unit.

Contents

Unit 13
Triads—1st Inversion 3
Triads—2nd Inversion 4
V^7 Chord—1st, 2nd and 3rd Inversions 5
Figured Bass 6
Major Chord Progressions 7
Unit 13 Test 8

Unit 14
Minor Scales 9
Natural, Harmonic and Melodic Minor Scales 10
Minor Triads 11
Augmented & Diminished Triads 12
Minor, Augmented and
   Diminished Triads Review 13
Unit 14 Test 14

Unit 15
The Primary Triads in Minor Keys 15
Minor Chord Progressions 16
Modes Related to the Major Scale:
   Ionian, Mixolydian, Lydian 17
Modes Related to the Major Scale:
   Ionian, Mixolydian, Lydian.
Modes Related to the Minor Scale:
   Aeolian, Dorian 18
Modes Related to the Minor Scale:
   Aeolian, Dorian, Phrygian, Locrian 19
Unit 15 Test 20

Unit 16
Harmonizing A Melody in a Major Key 21
Broken Chords & Arpeggiated Accompaniments 22
Passing & Neighboring Tones 23
Composing a Melody in a Major Key 24
Composing a Melody with Harmony in a Major Key ... 25
Unit 16 Test 26

Unit 17
Harmonizing a Melody in a Minor Key 27
Composing a Melody in a Minor Key 28
12-bar Blues Chord Progression 29
The Blues Scale 30
Composing and Harmonizing a Blues Melody 31
Unit 17 Test 32

Unit 18
Basic Forms of Music—Motive and Phrase 33
A B (Binary) Form 34
A B A (Ternary) Form 35
Rondo Form 36
Form Review 37
Unit 18 Test 38

Answer Keys 39–47

Grade Form 48

Unit 13 ACTIVITY 1 Name/Class_____

Use after completing page 83 of Alfred's Essentials of Music Theory, Book 3.

Triads—1st Inversion

1 Rewrite the following root position triads in open position. Use accidentals as needed.

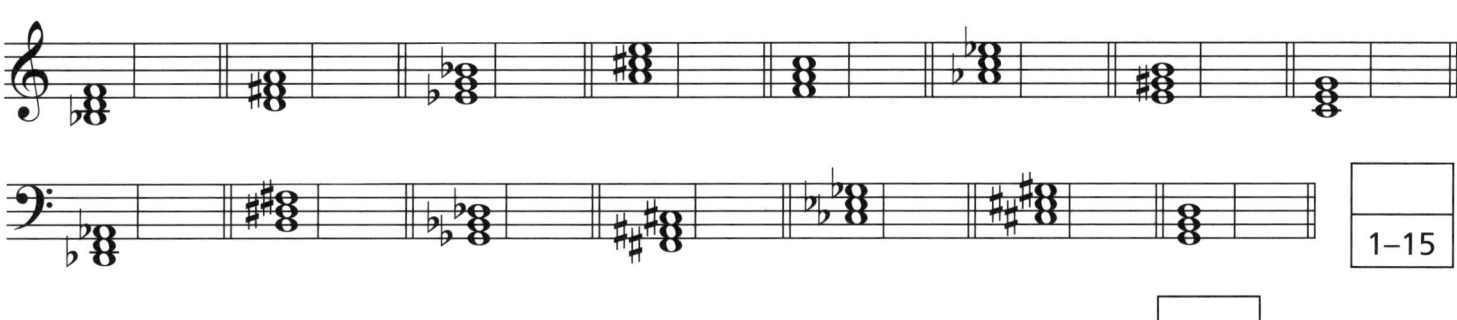

1–15

2 The bottom note in a first inversion triad is the _____.

10

3 Using the given notes as the root, add the 3rd and 5th *below* each note to make 1st inversion triads (close position). Use accidentals as needed.

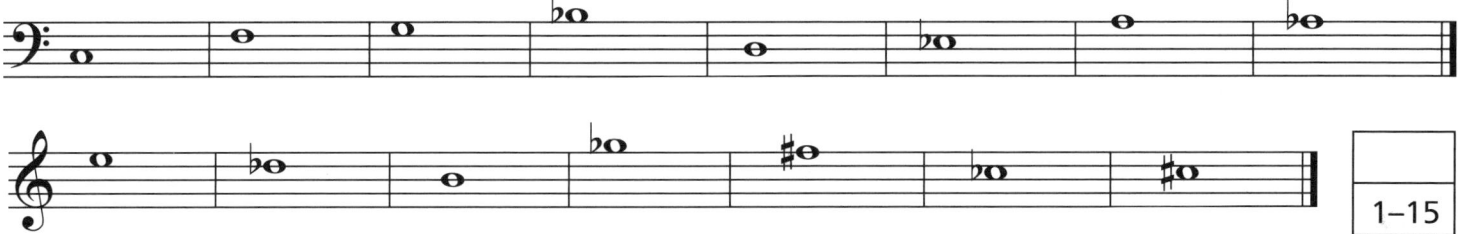

1–15

4 Using the given notes as the 3rd, add the 5th and root *above* each note to make 1st inversion triads (close position). Use accidentals as needed.

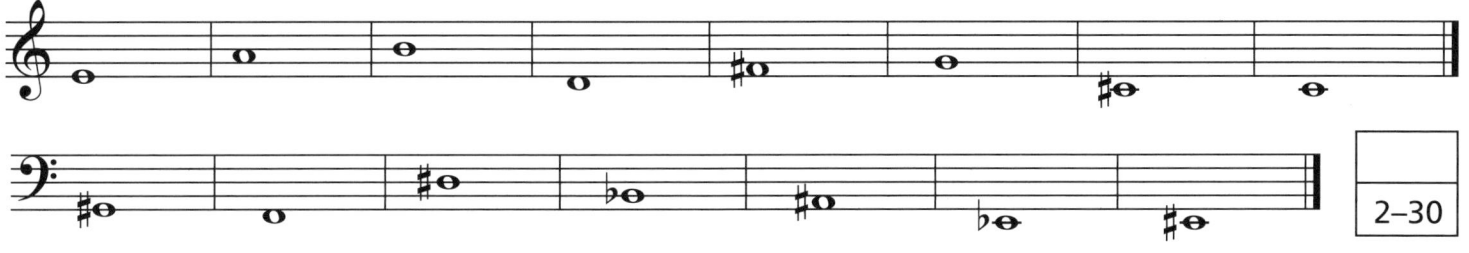

2–30

5 Rewrite the following root position triads in 1st inversion (close position). Use accidentals as needed.

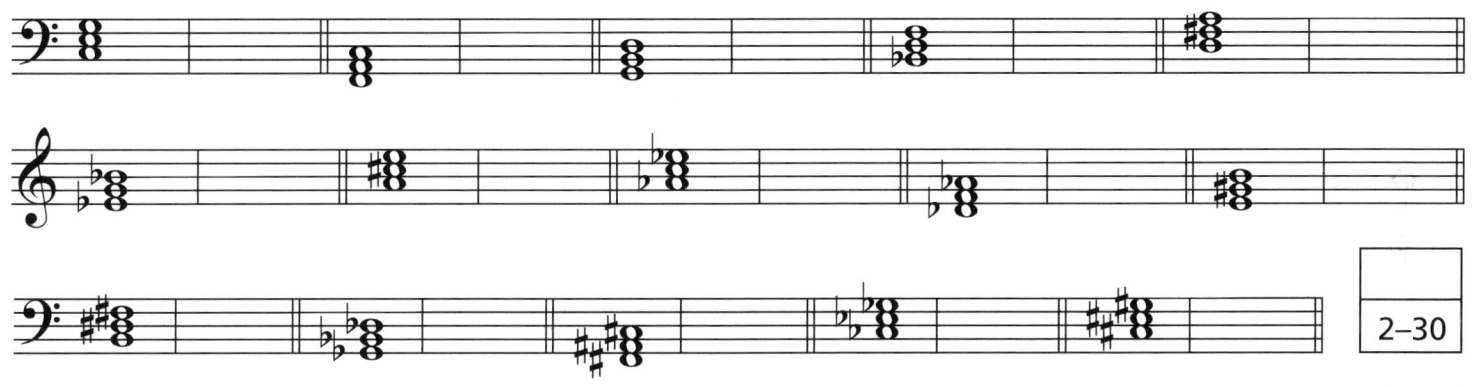

2–30

100

Alfred's Essentials of **MUSIC THEORY**

Teacher's Activity Kit, Book 3

30 Reproducible Activities, Plus 6 Tests

ANDREW SURMANI • KAREN FARNUM SURMANI • MORTON MANUS

Foreword

Alfred's Essentials of Music Theory, in books and software, has quickly become one of the most widely used theory courses. In order for students to learn new concepts thoroughly, however, it is necessary to repeat and reinforce those concepts in unique ways. The reproducible pages of Activities and Tests included in *Teacher's Activity Kit*, Book 3 will help every student become more familiar with concepts introduced in Book 3 of the *Alfred's Essentials of Music Theory* course.

Though correlated with *Alfred's Essentials of Music Theory*, Book 3, the materials in this kit may also be used to advantage with any theory text.

Unique features of *Teacher's Activity Kit*, Book 3:

Activities
There are five Activities in each of the six Units, which correlate specifically to the six Units in Book 3 of *Alfred's Essentials of Music Theory*. The wide variety of Activities includes Triad Inversions, Minor Scales, Augmented and Diminished Triads, Chord Progressions, Harmonization, Basic Forms of Music, and others for a total of 30 Activities in all.

Tests
There is one Test per Unit that covers all the theory concepts introduced in that Unit.

Scorekeeping
Each reproducible page includes scoring boxes to help the instructor grade the page.

Record Keeping
There is one reproducible Grade Form page, with a grid to keep track of the students' scores for every page in the Kit.

Answer Key
Answers for every Activity and Test page are included in a reduced size to assist in the grading process.

The *Teacher's Activity Kit* is the perfect "teacher saver" for days when a substitute is required—activities can be offered easily and as needed.

Permission to Reproduce
The Activity and Test pages in this Kit may be reproduced on any copier or duplicating machine. Permission to reproduce these pages by the classroom teacher for students is granted by purchase of this book. This permission does not include storage in a retrieval system or transmission in any form. Reproduction of these pages for an entire school or school system is prohibited.

Thanks to:
Bruce Goldes

Alfred Publishing Co., Inc.
16320 Roscoe Blvd., Suite 100
P.O. Box 10003
Van Nuys, CA 91410-0003
alfred.com

Copyright © MMVI by Alfred Publishing Co., Inc.
All rights reserved.   Printed in USA.
ISBN-10: 0-7390-4430-3
ISBN-13: 978-0-7390-4430-8

Unit 13 ACTIVITY 2   Name/Class_____

Use after completing page 84.

Triads—2nd Inversion

1 The bottom note in a second inversion triad is the_____.

2 Rewrite the following 2nd inversion triads in open position. Use accidentals as needed.

3 Using the given notes as the root, add the 5th *below* and the 3rd above to make 2nd inversion triads (close position). Use accidentals as needed.

4 Using the given notes as the 5th, add the root and 3rd *above* each note to make 2nd inversion triads (close position). Use accidentals as needed.

5 Rewrite the following root position triads in 2nd inversion (close position). Use accidentals as needed.

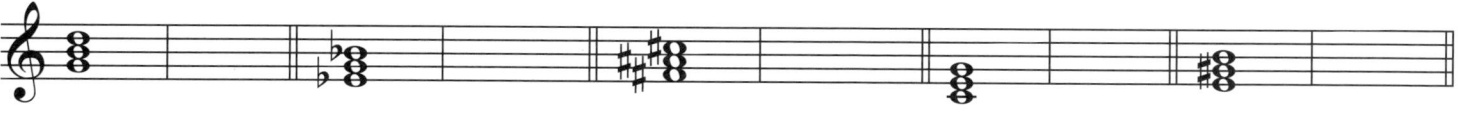

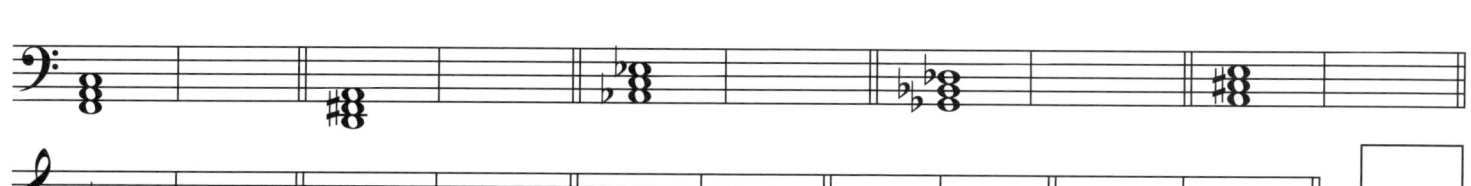

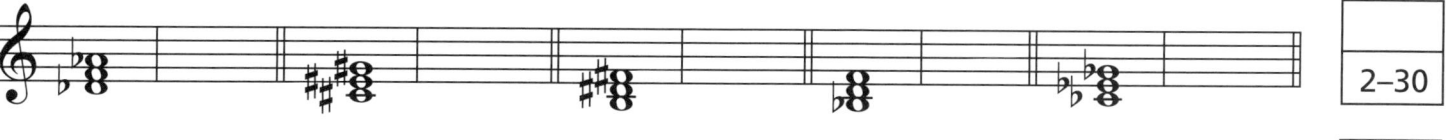

Copyright © MMVI by Alfred Publishing Co., Inc.

Unit 13 ACTIVITY 3 Name/Class_____

Use after completing page 85.

V7 Chord—1st, 2nd and 3rd Inversions

1 The bottom note in a 3rd inversion V7 chord is the _____.

2 Write the 1st, 2nd and 3rd inversions for the following V7 chords in close position.

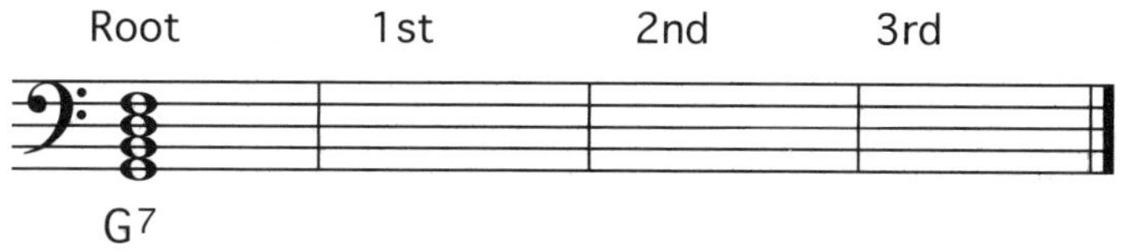

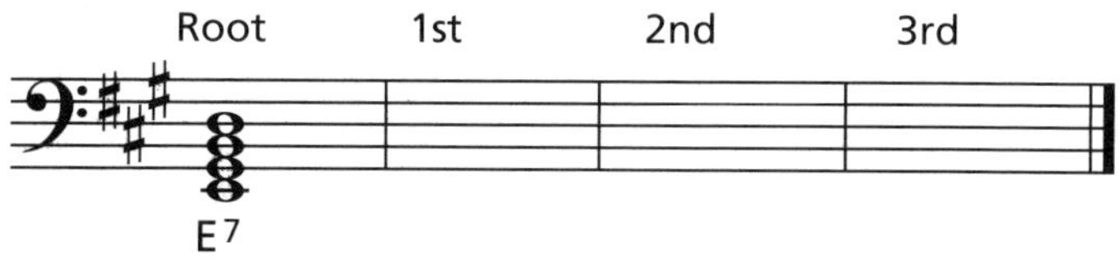

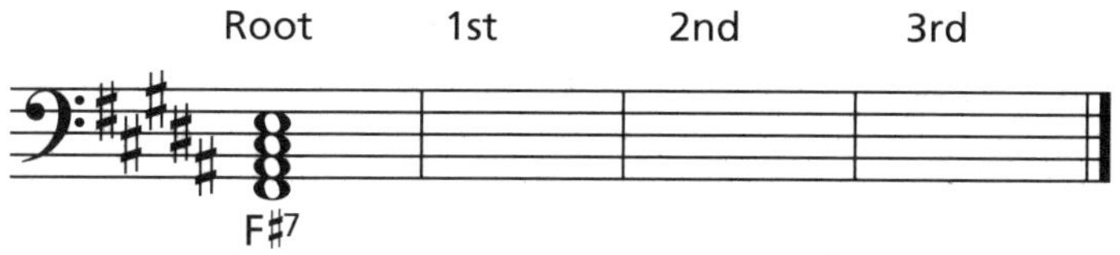

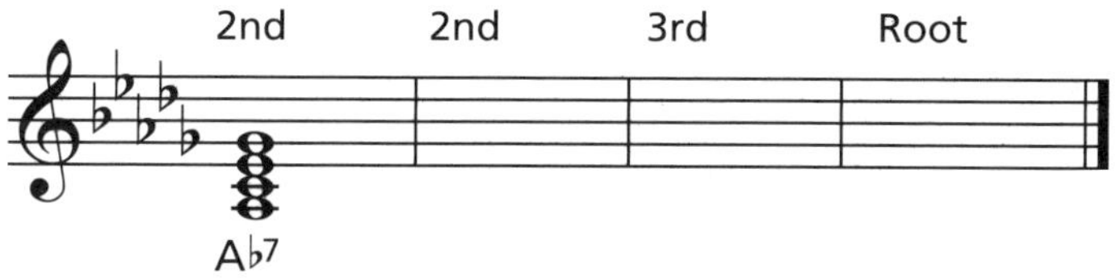

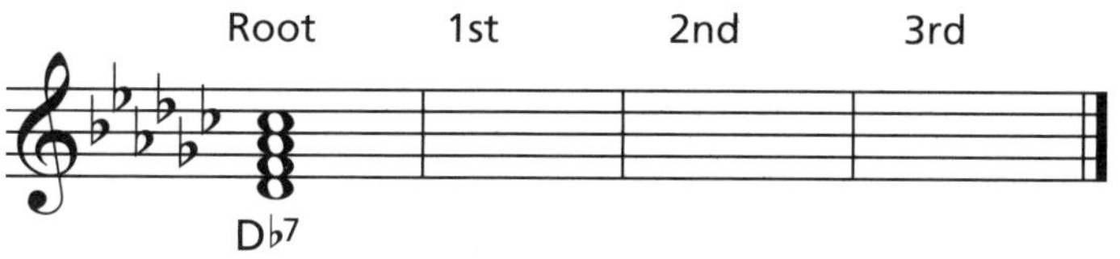

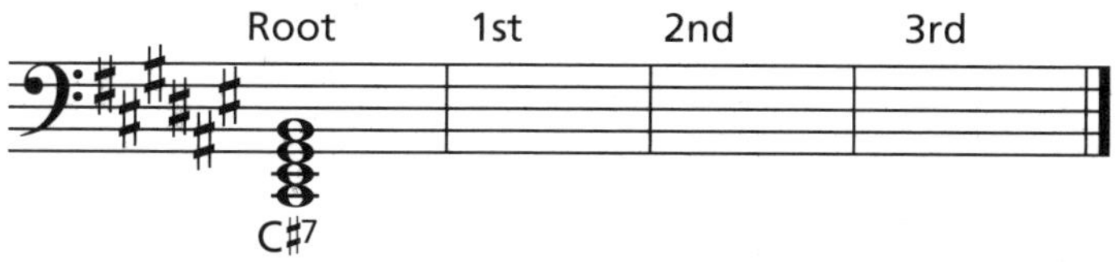

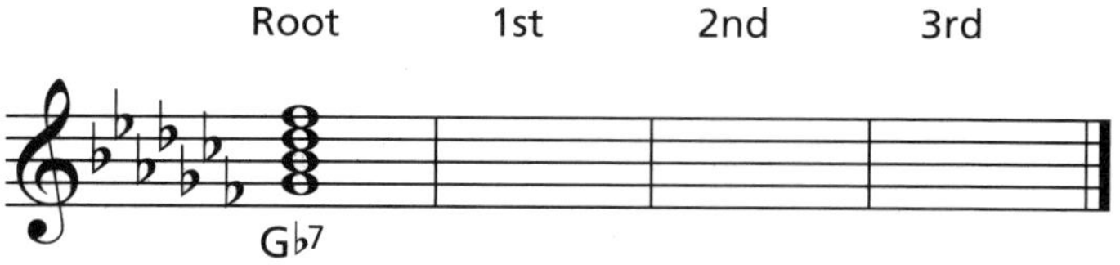

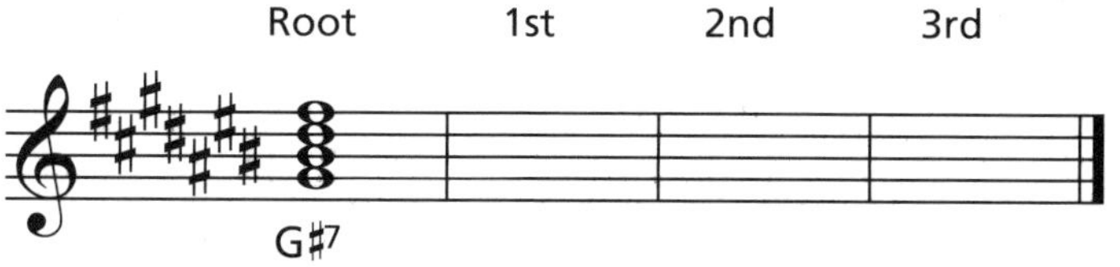

(G7, F#7, Ab7, Db7, C#7, G#7, E7, Bb7, Eb7, B7, Gb7)

3 Indicate the inversion of the following V7 chords (R, 1st, 2nd or 3rd).

Bb7, A7, C#7, Eb7, D7, F7, C7, B7

4 Write the following V7 chords in the given inversions using accidentals as needed.

G7 — 1st, Cb7 — 1st, Ab7 — 3rd, Db7 — 2nd, E7 — 3rd, F#7 — 1st, Gb7 — 2nd

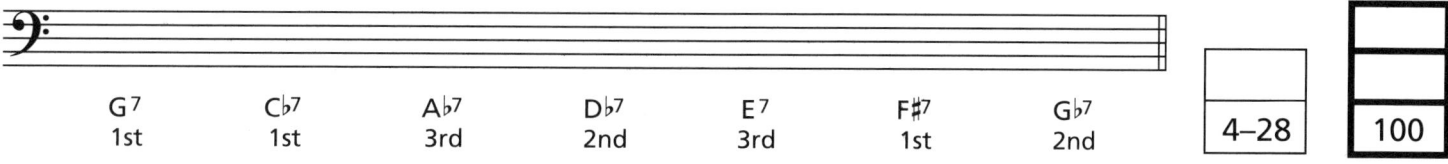

Copyright © MMVI by Alfred Publishing Co., Inc.

Unit 13 ACTIVITY 4 Name/Class_____

Use after completing page 86.

Figured Bass

1 Match the figured bass with the correct inversion.

I^6 _____   a. Dominant 7th chord, 1st inversion

V^4_3 _____   b. Dominant 7th chord, 2nd inversion

I^6_4 _____   c. Triad, 1st inversion

V^4_2 _____   d. Triad, 2nd inversion

V^6_5 _____   e. Dominant 7th chord, 3rd inversion

7–35

2 Write the chord symbol above the staff and the Roman numeral below the staff, using figured bass where applicable for each chord in the given keys.

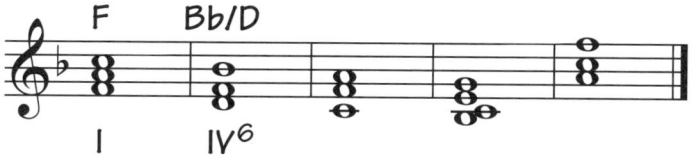
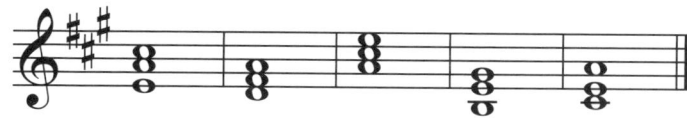

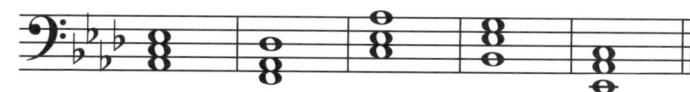

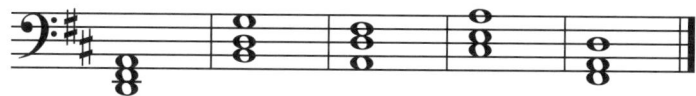

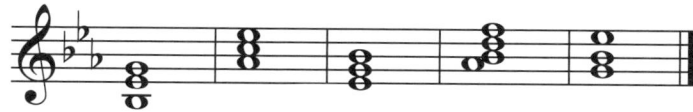
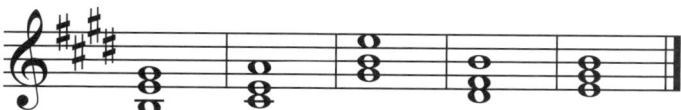

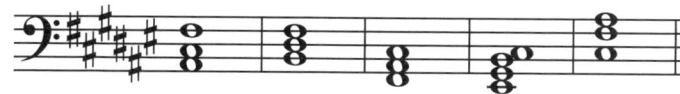
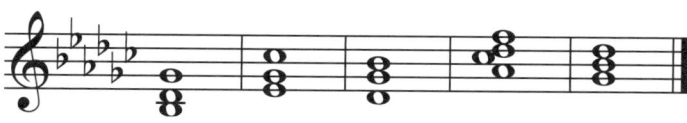

5–65   100

Unit 13 ACTIVITY 5   Name/Class_____

Use after completing page 87.

Major Chord Progressions

1 Chord progressions are used to _____ melodies.

2 The most common chords used in major chord progressions, because they contain all the notes of the major scale are the _____, _____, _____ and _____ chords.

3 Write the chord progression in each given key, using inversions as indicated for a smooth chord progression. Write the chord symbols above the staff.

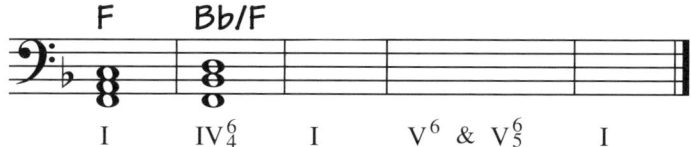

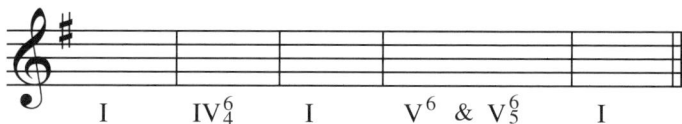
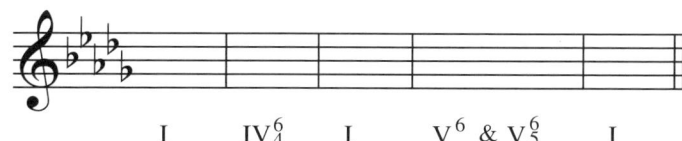
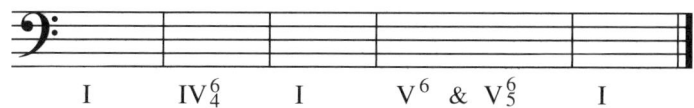

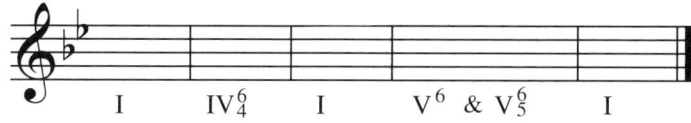

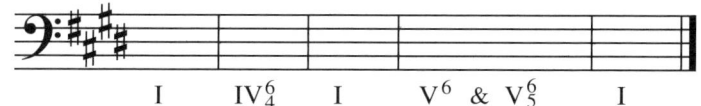
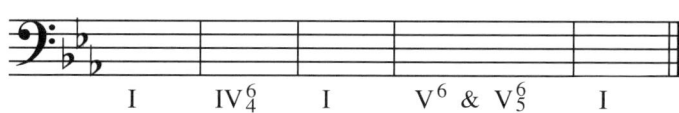

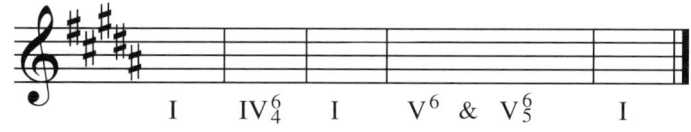
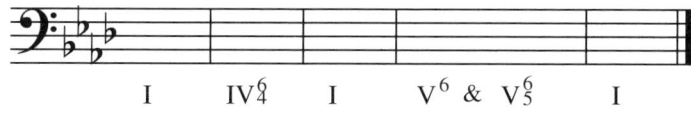
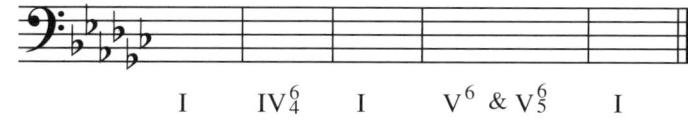
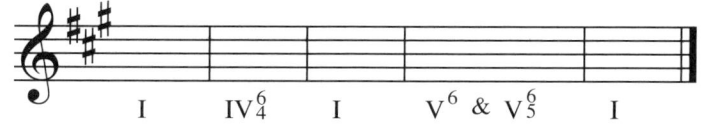
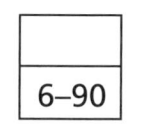

Copyright © MMVI by Alfred Publishing Co., Inc.

Unit 13 TEST Name/Class_____

Use after completing page 87.

1 Match the bottom note in the chord with the correct inversion.

    Root _____   a. 3rd inversion of V^7

    5th _____   b. 2nd inversion

    3rd _____   c. Root position

    7th _____   d. 1st inversion

4–16

2 Rewrite the following triads in open position.

Open Position

3–15

3 Rewrite the following triads in 1st inversion. Use open position. Add the chord symbols above the staff and the Roman numerals with figured bass below the staff.

Open Position

3–15

4 Rewrite the following triads in 2nd inversion. Use close position. Add the chord symbols above the staff and the Roman numerals with figured bass below the staff.

Close Position

3–15

5 Write the 1st, 2nd and 3rd inversions for the following V^7 chords. Use close position. Add the chord symbols above the staff and the Roman numerals below the staff.

Close Position Bb7   **Close Position** F#7

        V^7 V

4–24

6 Rewrite the following chord progression using inversions so it sounds smoother. Add the chord symbols above the staff and the Roman numerals below the staff.

    Ab   Db   Ab   Eb   Ab

    I   IV   I V^7 I

3–15

100

Copyright © MMVI by Alfred Publishing Co., Inc.

Unit 14 ACTIVITY 1 Name/Class_____

Use after completing page 90.

Minor Scales

1. To find the keynote of the relative minor scale from the keynote of the major scale, ascend / descend (circle one) a minor third.   20

2. To find the keynote of the relative major scale from the keynote of the minor scale, ascend / descend (circle one) a minor third.   20

3. Write the major and minor key names under each key signature.

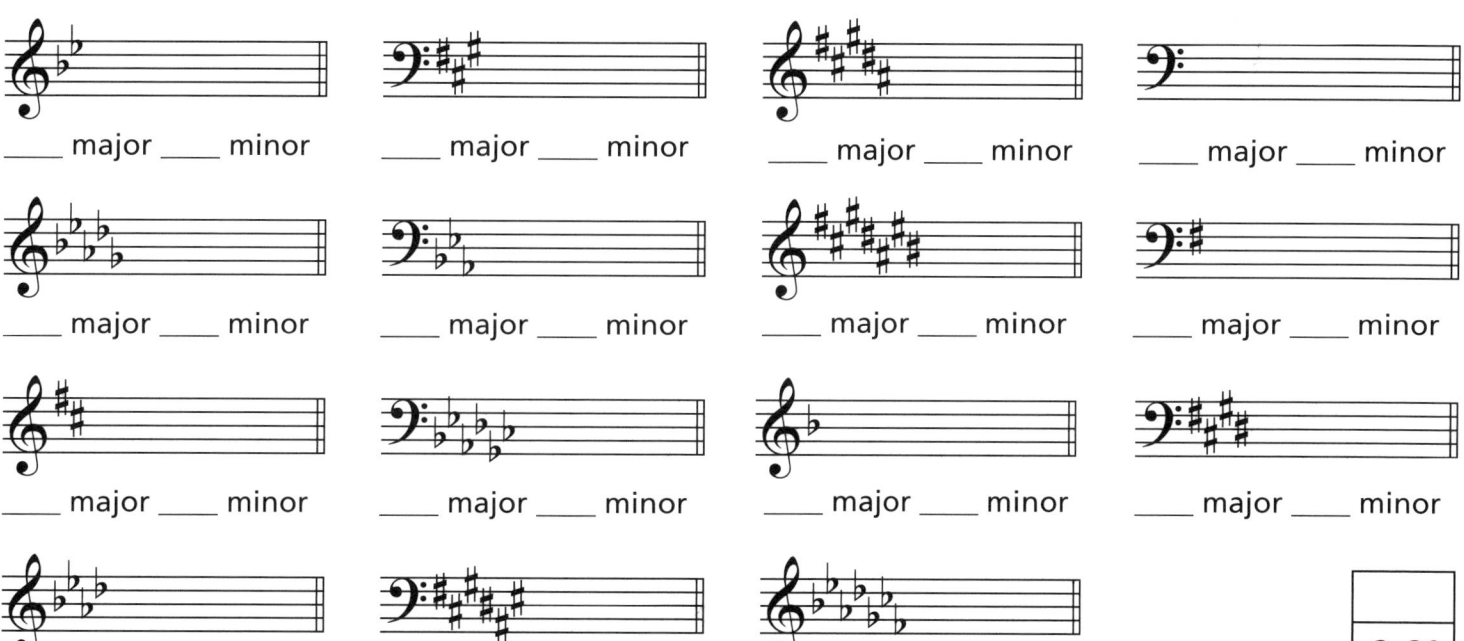

4. Write the following major key signatures and scales using quarter notes.

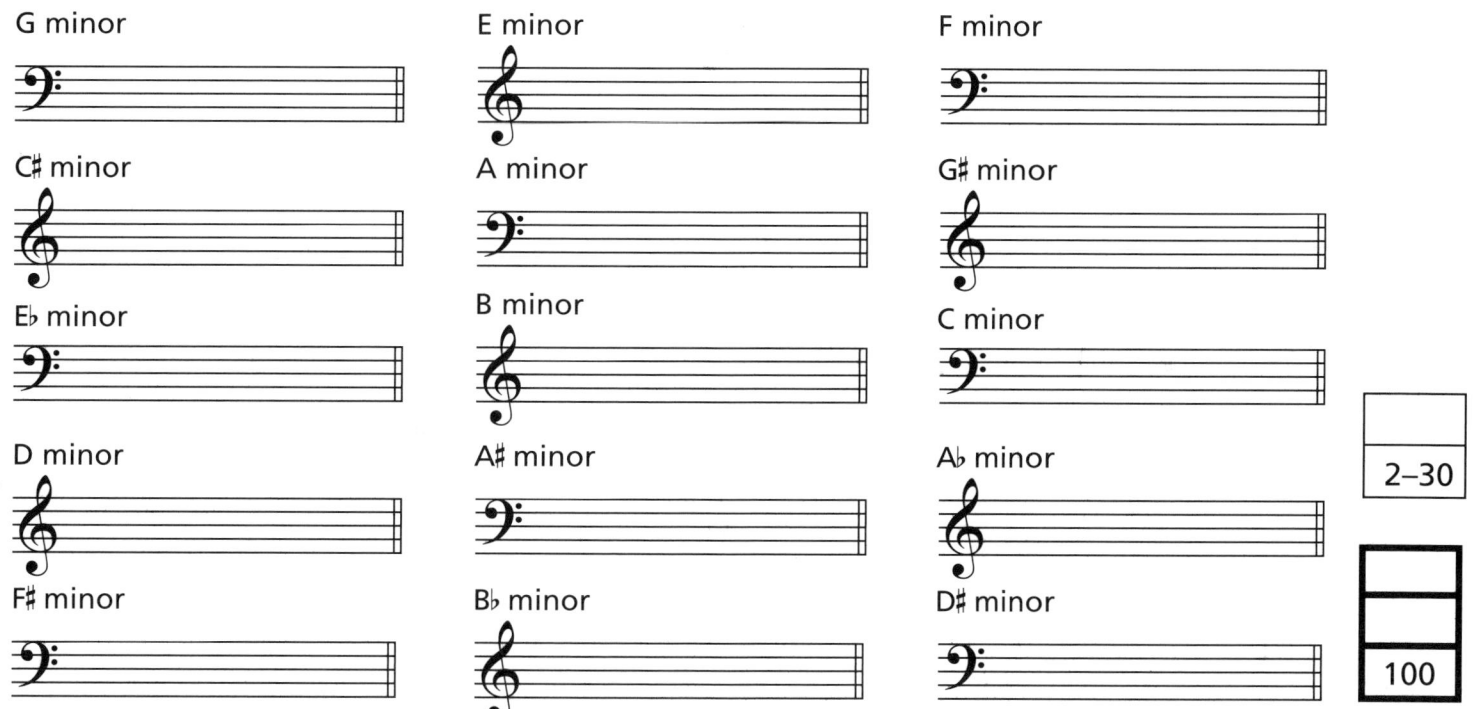

Unit 14 **ACTIVITY 2**   Name/Class_____

Use after completing page 91.

Natural, Harmonic and Melodic Minor Scales

1 The relative minor scale begins on the _____ note of the relative major scale. | 8 |

2 Fill in the blanks with the correct minor scale.

a. The 7th tone is raised by a half step ascending and descending: _____.

b. It uses only the tones of the relative major scale: _____.

c. The 6th and 7th tones are raised by a half step ascending,
but descend like the natural minor scale: _____. | 7–21 |

3 Add key signatures and write the following minor scales using quarter notes.

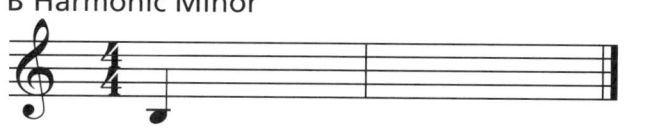
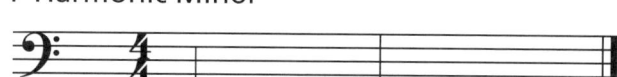

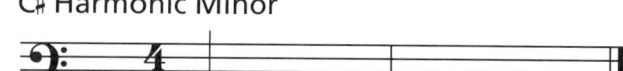

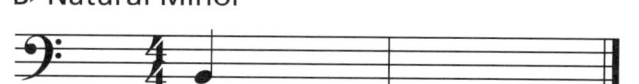
| .5–24 |

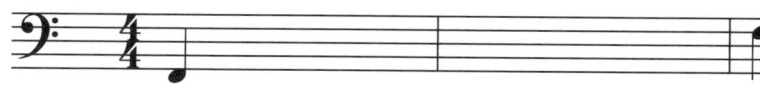
| .5–15 |

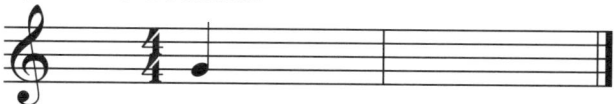

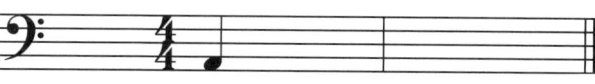
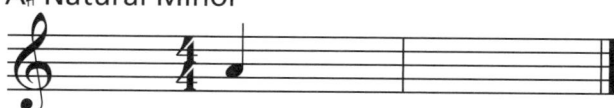
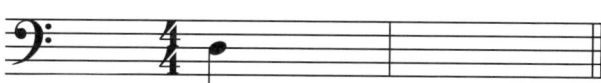
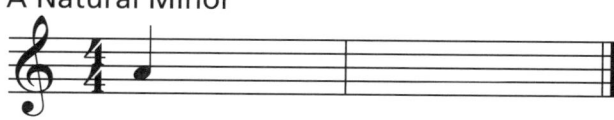

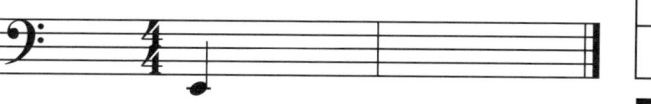
| .5–24 |

| .5–8 |
| 100 |

Copyright © MMVI by Alfred Publishing Co., Inc.

Unit 14 **ACTIVITY 3** Name/Class_____

Use after completing page 92.

Minor Triads

1 Minor triads consist of a root,_____3rd and a perfect 5th.

2 Build a minor triad by adding a_____3rd on top of a_____3rd.

3 Write the name of each minor triad.

4 Write the following minor triads, adding accidentals where applicable.

Dm   F#m   E♭m   A♭m   D#m   Gm   Em   Am

C#m   Fm   B♭m   Cm   A#m   Bm   G#m

5 Label each triad in the keys of E♭ and A major using upper case Roman numerals for major, and lower case for minor.

Copyright © MMVI by Alfred Publishing Co., Inc.

Unit 14 **ACTIVITY 4** Name/Class_____

Use after completing page 93.

Augmented and Diminished Triads

1. To create an augmented triad from a major triad, (circle one) **raise / lower**
   the (circle one) **root   3rd   5th**   by a half step.

2. An augmented triad is built by adding a_____3rd on top of a_____3rd.

3. To create a diminished triad from a minor triad, (circle one) **raise / lower**
   the (circle one) **root   3rd   5th**   by a half step.

4. A diminished triad is built by adding a_____3rd on top of a_____3rd.

5. In the major scale, a triad built on the _____ scale degree is diminished.

6. Write the name of each augmented triad.

7. Write the name of each diminished triad.

8. Create triads from the given chord name.

G+   C#°   Bb°   F+   A+   C°   G°   Ab°

Db+   E°   Gb+   F#°   D+   B°   Eb°

Copyright © MMVI by Alfred Publishing Co., Inc.

Unit 14 ACTIVITY 5 Name/Class_____

Use after completing page 93.

Minor, Augmented and Diminished Triads Review

1 Draw a line to match each of the following:

Root, minor 3rd, perfect 5th	Major triad
Root, minor 3rd, diminished 5th	Minor triad
Root, major 3rd, augmented 5th	Augmented triad
Root, major 3rd, perfect 5th	Diminished triad

.5–2

2 Label each triad using upper and lower case Roman numerals. Indicate if any chords are augmented (+) or diminished (°).

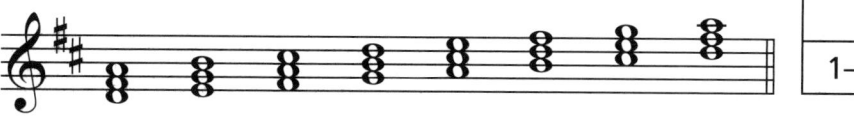

1–8

3 Write the following minor, augmented and diminished triads, using accidentals.

1–45

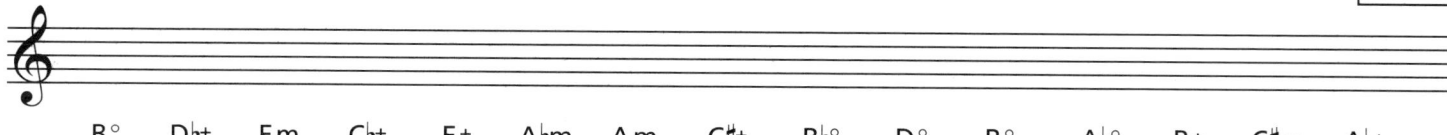

B° D♭+ Em C♭+ E+ A♭m Am C♯+ B♭° D° B° A♭° B+ C♯m A♭+

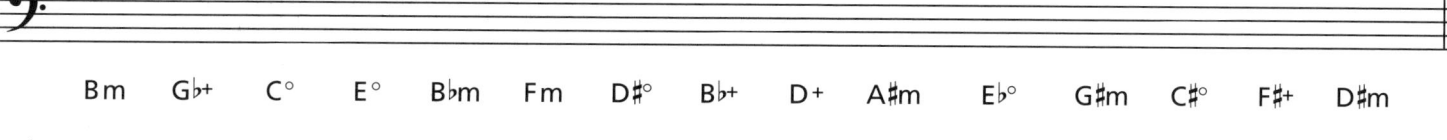

Bm G♭+ C° E° B♭m Fm D♯° B♭+ D+ A♯m E♭° G♯m C♯° F♯+ D♯m

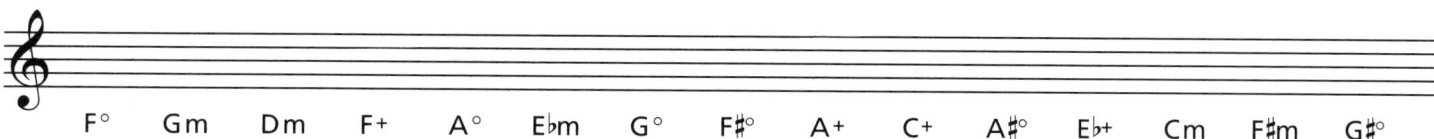

F° Gm Dm F+ A° E♭m G° F♯° A+ C+ A♯° E♭+ Cm F♯m G♯°

4 Write the name of each triad and indicate whether it is minor (m), augmented (+) or diminished (°).

1–45

100

Copyright © MMVI by Alfred Publishing Co., Inc.

Unit 14 TEST Name/Class_____

Use after completing page 93.

1 Write the relative major key name and the key signature for each minor key.

B minor: ____ major   C minor: ____ major   B♭ minor: ____ major   F♯ minor: ____ major

D minor: ____ major   A minor: ____ major   E♭ minor: ____ major   G minor: ____ major

[2–16]

2 Write the following minor scales with key signatures using quarter notes. Add accidentals where applicable.

C Natural Minor (ascending)   (descending)

B Melodic Minor (ascending)   (descending)

F Harmonic Minor (ascending)   (descending)

[.5–21]

3 Write the following minor triads using accidentals.

C♯m   Em   D♯m   Bm   A♯m

[3–15]

4 Write the following augmented triads using accidentals.

G+   D♭+   A+   F+   C♯+

[3–15]

5 Write the following diminished triads using accidentals.

A♭°   G♯°   D°   A♯°   C°

[3–15]

6 Fill in the missing triads from the 2nd scale degree to the 7th scale degree. Write the chord name above the staff (using the chord letter, m, +, or °) and the upper or lower case Roman numeral below the staff.

D♭ ____ ____ ____ ____ ____ D♭

I ____ ____ ____ ____ ____ I

[3–18]

[100]

Copyright © MMVI by Alfred Publishing Co., Inc.

Unit 15 Activity 1 Name/Class_____

Use after completing page 96.

The Primary Triads in Minor Keys

1 The primary triads in a minor key are built on the ____, ____ and ____ scale degrees.

2 In the harmonic minor scale, the _____ tone is raised a half step.

3 In the harmonic minor scale, the triads built on the:
- 1st and 4th scale degrees are _____ triads
- 5th and 6th scale degrees are _____ triads
- 2nd and 7th scale degrees are _____ triads
- 3rd scale degree is an _____ triad

4 For each example, name the minor key, and write the primary triads in root position. Use the harmonic minor scale. Use accidentals as needed.

Key of: __A minor__

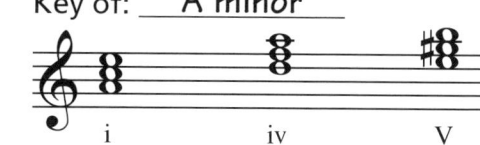

Key of: _____

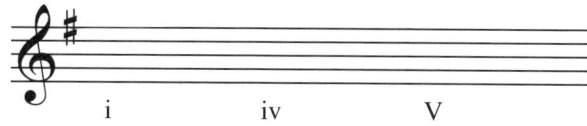

Key of: _____

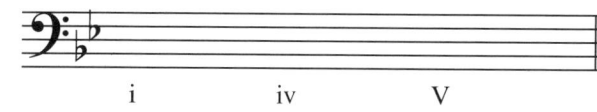

Key of: _____

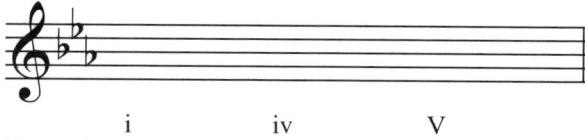

Key of: _____

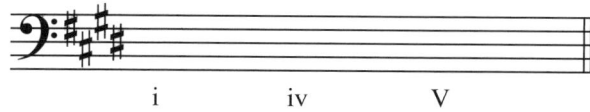

Key of: _____

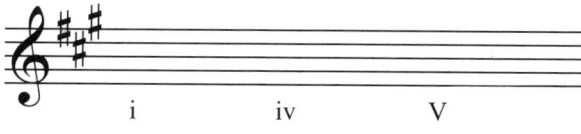

Key of: _____

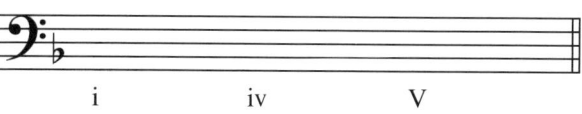

Key of: _____

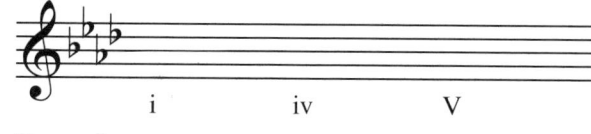

Key of: _____

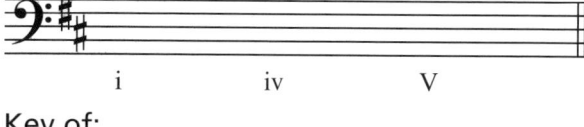

Key of: _____

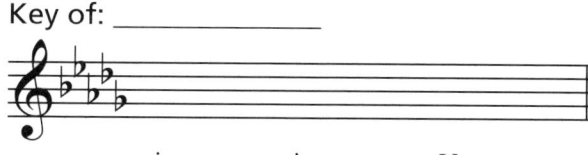

Key of: _____

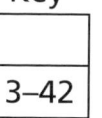

Copyright © MMVI by Alfred Publishing Co., Inc.

Unit 15 ACTIVITY 2 Name/Class_____

Use after completing page 97.

Minor Chord Progressions

1 The most common chords used in minor chord progressions, because they contain all the notes of the harmonic minor scale, are _____, _____, _____ and _____ chords.

2 To achieve a smoother chord progression (common tone between each chord), the iv chord is used in the _____ inversion and the V or V⁷ chord is used in the _____ inversion.

3 Write the key name above each example. Then, write the chords in each measure. Use the harmonic minor scale. Write the chord symbol for each above the staff.

Key of: _____

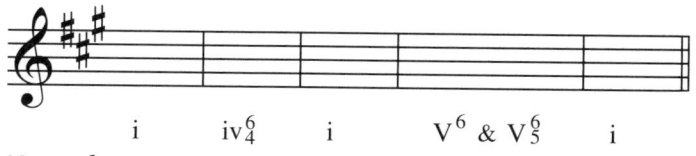

Key of: _____

Key of: _____

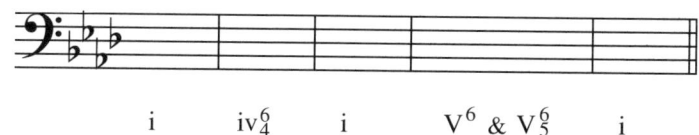

Key of: _____

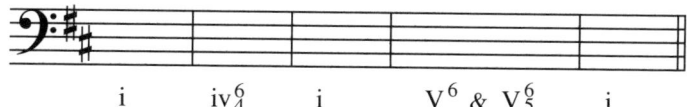

Key of: _____

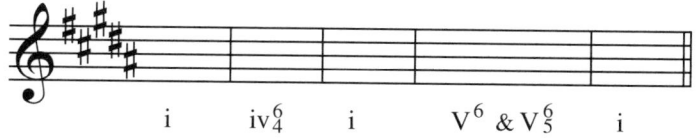

Key of: _____

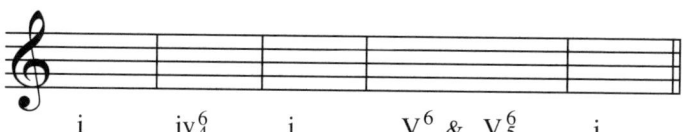

Key of: _____

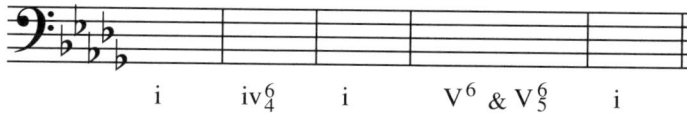

Key of: _____

Key of: _____

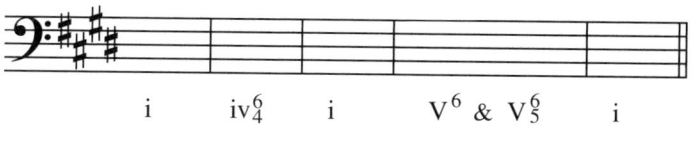

Key of: _____

Key of: _____

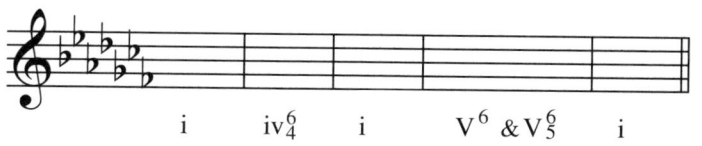

Key of: _____

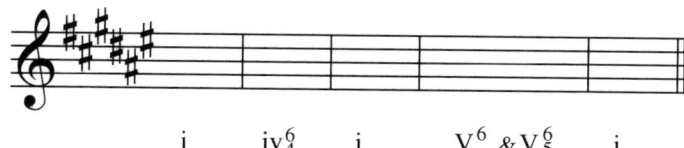

Unit 15 ACTIVITY 3 Name/Class_____

Use after completing page 98.

Modes Related to the Major Scale — *Ionian, Mixolydian, Lydian*

1 The modes related to major are _____, _____ and _____.

3–9

2 Write the key signature and notes for each mode using quarter notes. Add the appropriate accidentals.

E Lydian

B Ionian

A Mixolydian

A♭ Mixolydian

B♭ Lydian

A♭ Ionian

B Mixolydian

E♭ Lydian

E♭ Mixolydian

E Ionian

G♭ Lydian

D Ionian

B♭ Mixolydian

B♭ Ionian

G♭ Mixolydian

A Lydian

D Lydian

D♭ Ionian

A♭ Lydian

G♭ Ionian

D Mixolydian

A Ionian

E Mixolydian

B Lydian

D♭ Mixolydian

D♭ Lydian

E♭ Ionian

Unit 15 ACTIVITY 4 Name/Class_____

Use after completing page 99.

Modes Related to the Major Scale — *Ionian, Mixolydian, Lydian*
Modes Related to the Minor Scale — *Aeolian, Dorian*

1 The modes related to minor are **Aeolian**, _____, _____, and _____.

2 Write the key signature and notes for each mode using quarter notes. Add the appropriate accidentals.

Copyright © MMVI by Alfred Publishing Co., Inc.

Unit 15 **ACTIVITY 5** Name/Class_____

Use after completing page 99.

Modes Related to the Minor Scale—Aeolian, Dorian, Phrygian, Locrian

1 Draw lines to match the mode with its relative structure:

- Phrygian — natural minor scale with a raised 6th scale degree
- Locrian — natural minor scale
- Aeolian — natural minor scale with a lowered 2nd scale degree
- Dorian — natural minor scale with lowered 2nd and 5th scale degrees

2 Write the key signature and notes for each mode using quarter notes. Add the appropriate accidentals.

C# Aeolian

F# Phrygian

A# Locrian

A Phrygian

C Locrian

G# Phrygian

B Locrian

D# Locrian

B Phrygian

A Locrian

F Phrygian

E Locrian

C Phrygian

F# Locrian

D# Phrygian

A# Phrygian

C# Locrian

E♭ Phrygian

B Locrian

B Phrygian

E♭ Locrian

C# Phrygian

G# Locrian

D Locrian

G Locrian

G Phrygian

Unit 15 TEST Name/Class_____

Use after completing page 99.

1 In the harmonic minor scale, the _____ and _____ triads are minor triads.

2 In the harmonic minor scale, the _____ and _____ triads are major triads.

3 In the harmonic minor scale, the _____ and _____ triads are diminished triads.

4 In the harmonic minor scale, the _____ triad is an augmented triad.

2–8

5 Write all the chords for each example using the harmonic minor scale. Write the chord symbols above the staff, indicating whether the chord is major (chord letter), minor (m), augmented (+) or diminished (°). Write the Roman numerals below the staff using upper case for Major and Augmented, and lower case for minor and diminished. Indicate which chords are Augmented (+) or diminished (°).

24–48

C# minor

C minor

6 For each example, name the minor key, and write the primary chords using a smooth chord progression. Include the figured bass. Write the chord symbols above the staff.

12–24

Key of: _____

Key of: _____

i   iv   i   V   i

i   iv   i   V   i

7 When moving from a i chord in root position to a iv chord, the smoothest progression has the iv chord in _____ inversion.

4

8 Draw lines to match the mode with its relative structure:

Dorian mode — major scale with the 4th raised a half step
Mixolydian mode — major scale with 7th lowered a half step
Locrian mode — minor scale with the 6th raised a half step
Ionian mode — minor scale with the 2nd lowered a half step
Phrygian mode — major scale with no alterations
Aeolian mode — minor scale with the 2nd & 5th lowered a half step
Lydian mode — natural minor scale with no alterations

1–7

9 Write the key signature and notes for the following mode. Add the appropriate accidentals.

Bb Dorian

1–9

100

Copyright © MMVI by Alfred Publishing Co., Inc.

Unit 16 **ACTIVITY 1** Name/Class_____

Use after completing page 102.

Harmonizing a Melody in a Major Key

1 Indicate which scale degrees harmonize with the following major chords:

I chord _____   IV chord _____   V or V⁷ chord _____

1–3

2 Which chord tone can be omitted when harmonizing with the V⁷ chord? _____

1

3 Harmonize the exercises with the I, IV, V (and V⁷) chords using inversions where necessary, to achieve a smooth progression between chords. Write the chord symbols above the staff and the Roman numerals below the staff for each chord.

24–96

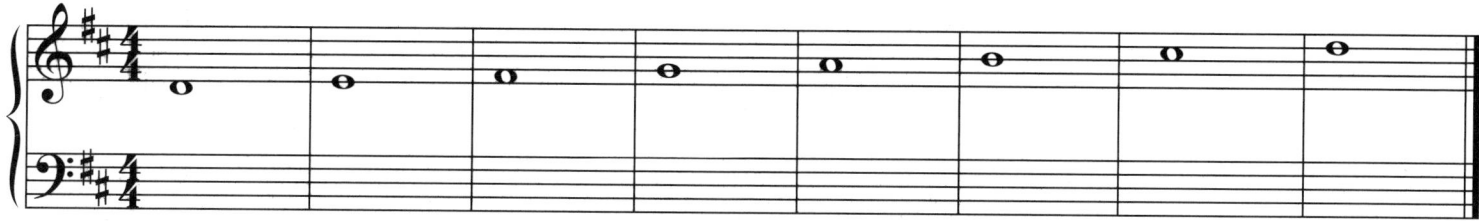

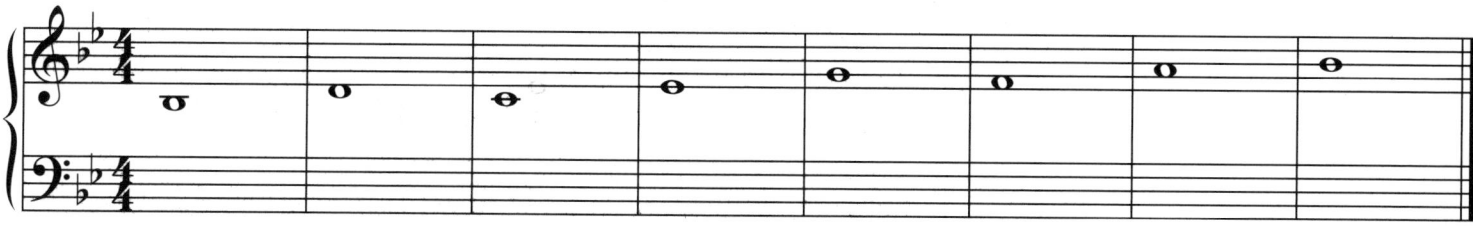

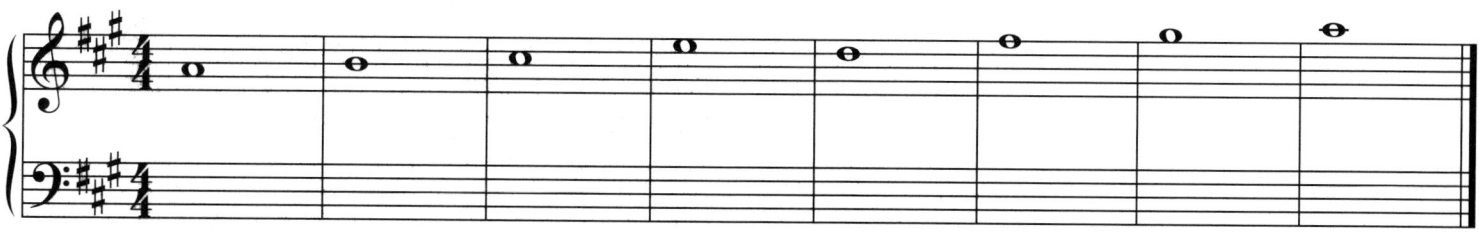

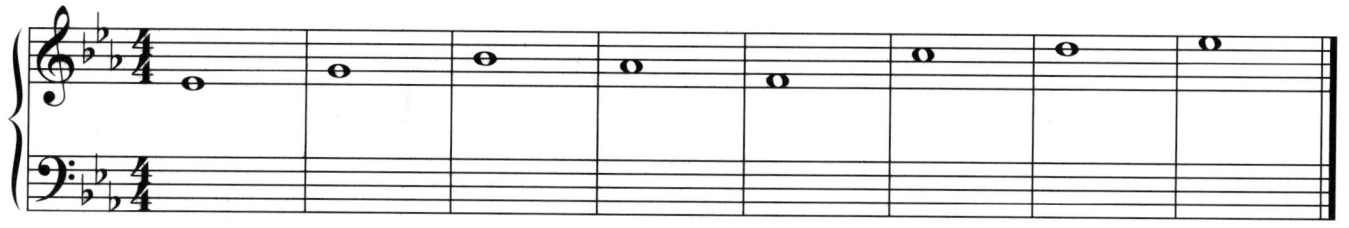

100

Copyright © MMVI by Alfred Publishing Co., Inc.

Unit 16 ACTIVITY 4 Name/Class_____

Use after completing page 105.

Composing a Melody in a Major Key

1 Analyze the harmony provided in the following examples. Write the Roman numerals below the staff, then add the chord symbols above the staff. Write a melody and circle any non-harmonic tones, indicating whether they are passing (P), upper neighboring (U), or lower neighboring tones (L).

a.

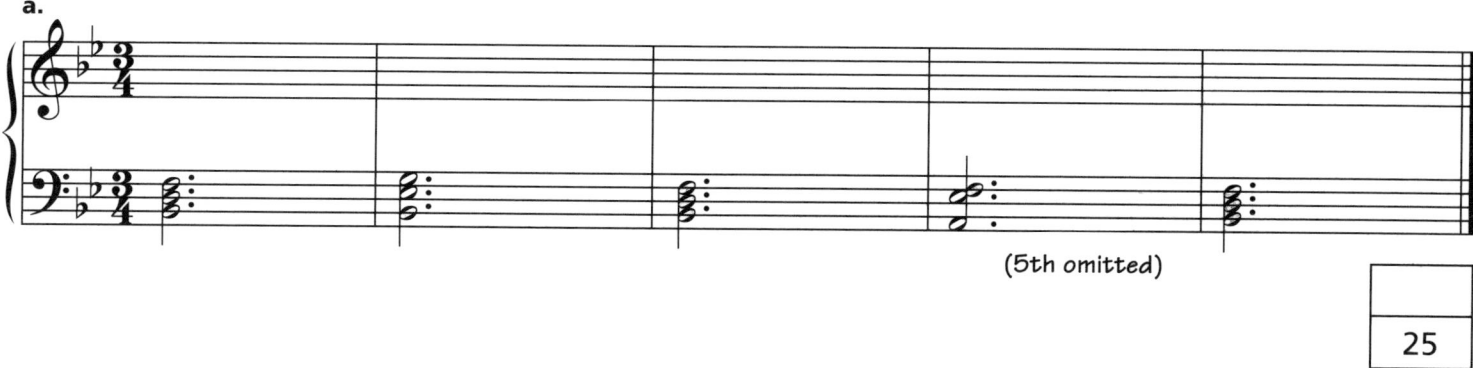

(5th omitted)

25

b.

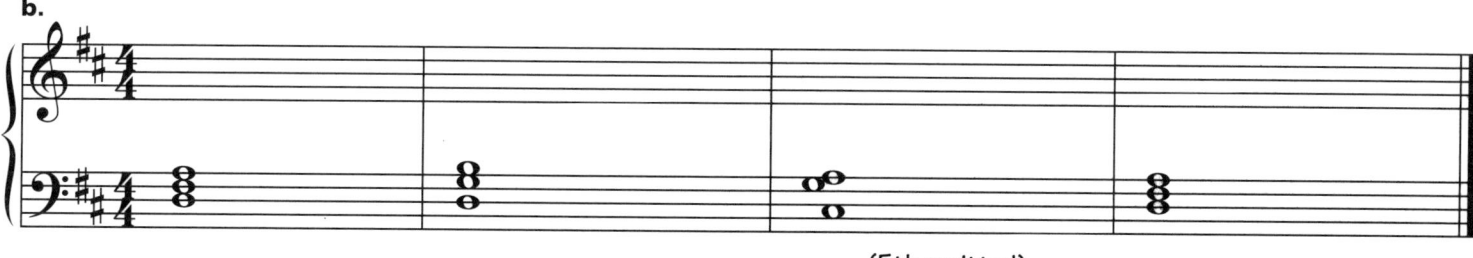

(5th omitted)

25

c.

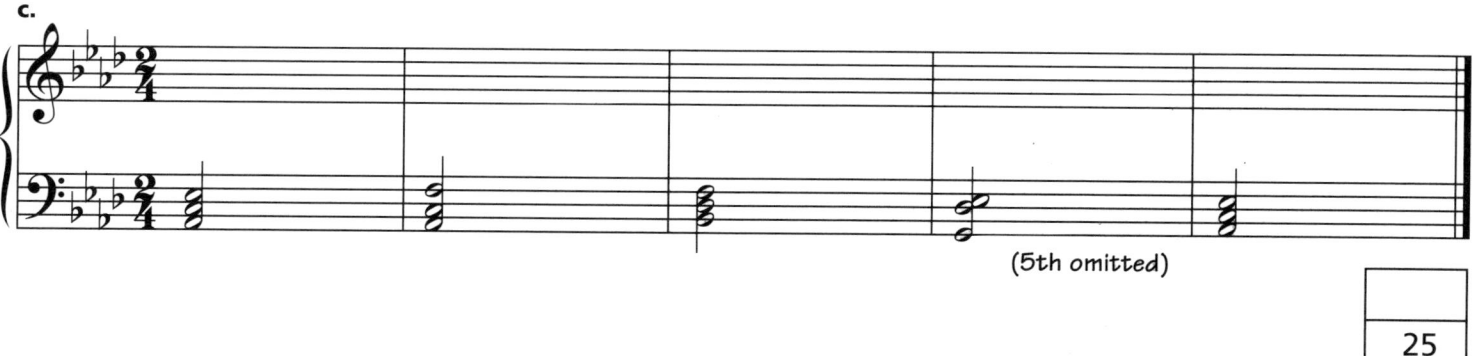

(5th omitted)

25

d.

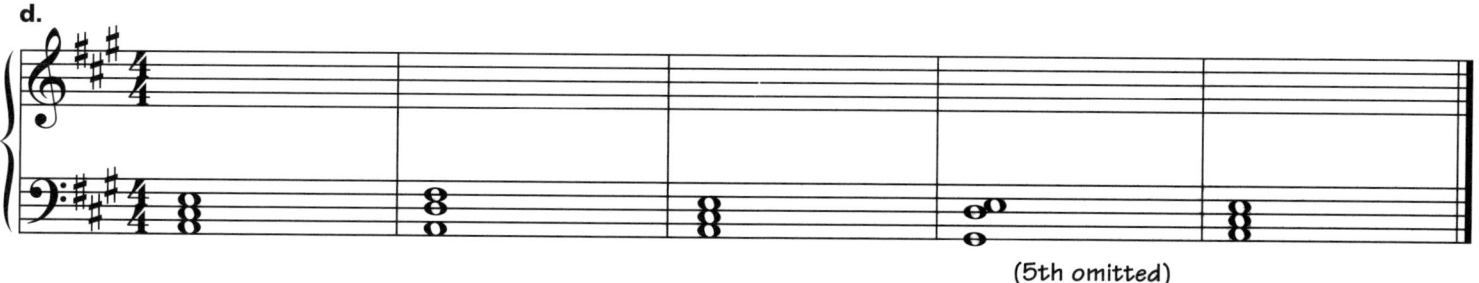

(5th omitted)

25 | 100

Copyright © MMVI by Alfred Publishing Co., Inc.

Unit 16 ACTIVITY 5 Name/Class _____

Use after completing page 105.

Composing a Melody with Harmony in a Major Key

1 Write a 16-bar melody in a major key. Indicate the key signature and time signature at the beginning of the piece. Next, harmonize the melody using **both** block chords and broken chords. Circle the non-harmonic tones and indicate whether they are passing (P), upper neighboring (U) or lower neighboring tones (L).

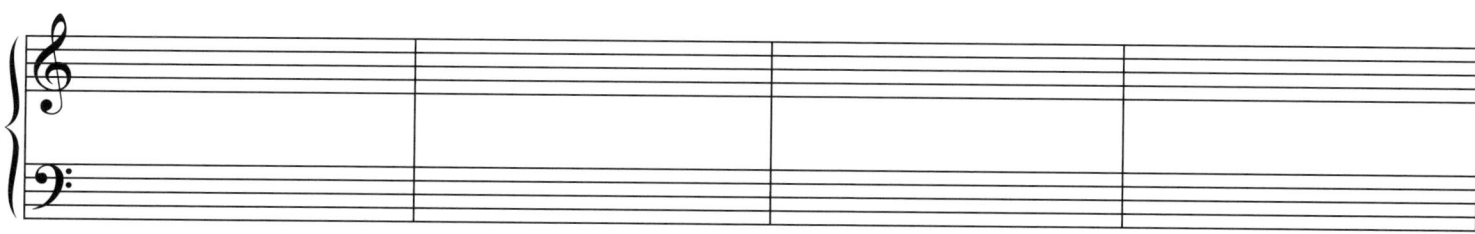

Time Sig.–5
Key Sig.–5
Harmony–25
N.H. Tones–15
Melody–50

100

Copyright © MMVI by Alfred Publishing Co., Inc.

Unit 16 TEST Name/Class_____

Use after completing page 105.

1 Harmonize the following melody with one chord in each measure. Using I, IV and V⁷ chords with inversions as needed to create smooth progression between chords, write the chord symbols above the staff and the Roman numerals below the staff for each chord.

Chord Sym.–8
Roman Num.–8
Chords–12

Risseldy Rosseldy

American Folk Song

2 Add an arpeggiated accompaniment to the following melody. Write the chord symbols above the staff and the Roman numerals below the staff for each chord.

Sehnsucht

Franz Schubert (1797–1828)

16

3 In the following melody, circle the non-harmonic tones and indicate whether they are passing (P), upper neighboring (U) or lower neighboring tones (L).

Deta, Deta

Japanese Folk Song

5–25

4 Analyze the harmony provided. Write the Roman numerals below the staff, then add the chord symbols above the staff. Write a melody, then circle and label any non-harmonic tones used.

Chord Sym.–5
Roman Num.–5
Melody–15
N.H. Tones–6

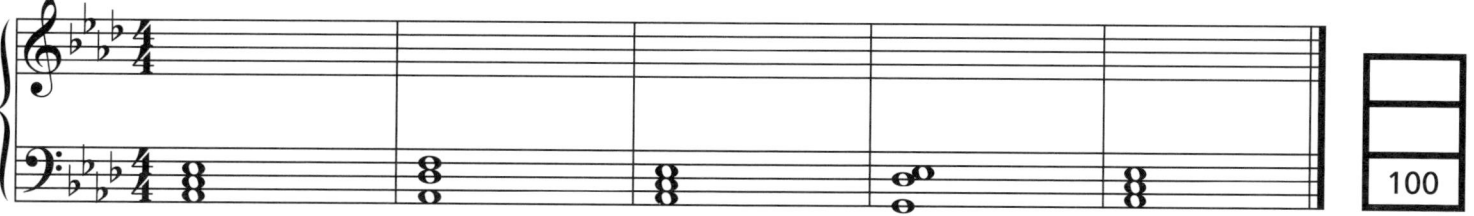

100

Copyright © MMVI by Alfred Publishing Co., Inc.

Unit 17 ACTIVITY 1 Name/Class_____

Use after completing page 108.

Harmonizing a Melody in a Minor Key

1 Indicate which scale degree tones would harmonize with the following minor chords:

    i chord _____   iv chord _____   V or V⁷ chord _____

3–9

2 Which minor scale is most commonly used when harmonizing a melody in a minor key?
_____

3

3 Harmonize the B harmonic minor scale with the i, iv, V (and V⁷) chords using inversions where necessary, to achieve a smooth progression between chords. Write the chord symbols above the staff and the Roman numerals below the staff for each chord, using figured bass.

1–8

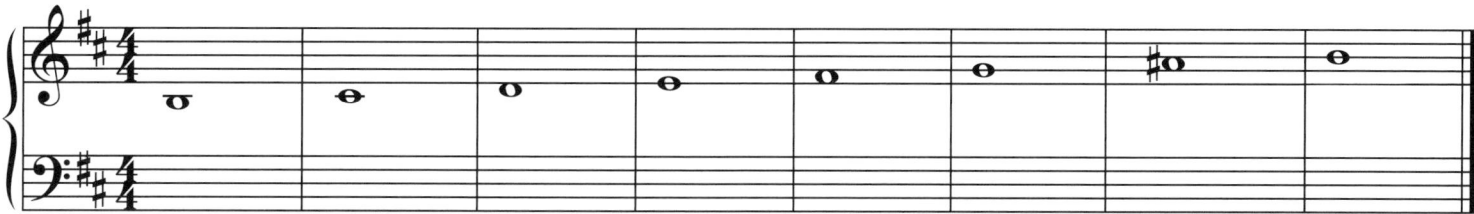

4 Harmonize the following minor melodies using the given chord symbols. Circle the non-harmonic tones and indicate whether they are passing (P), upper neighboring (U) or lower neighboring tones (L).

Chords: 4–36
N.H. Tones: 1.5–7.5

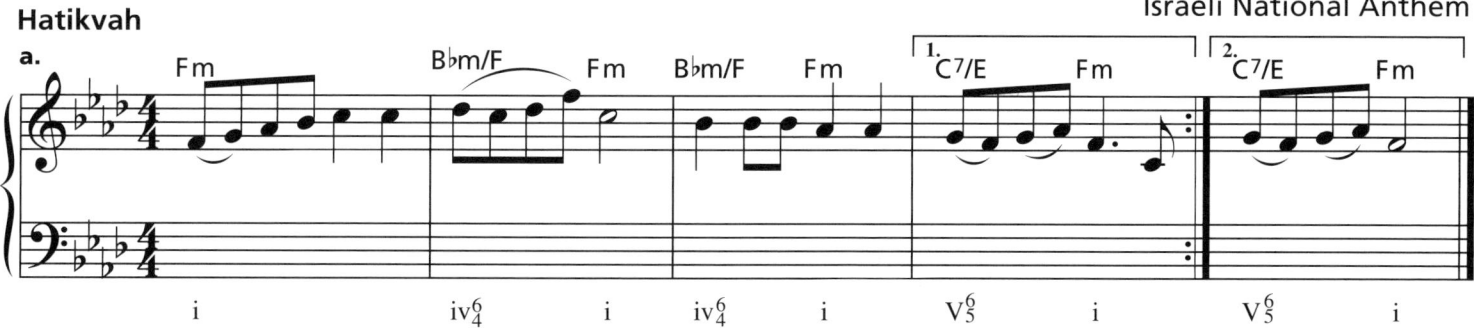

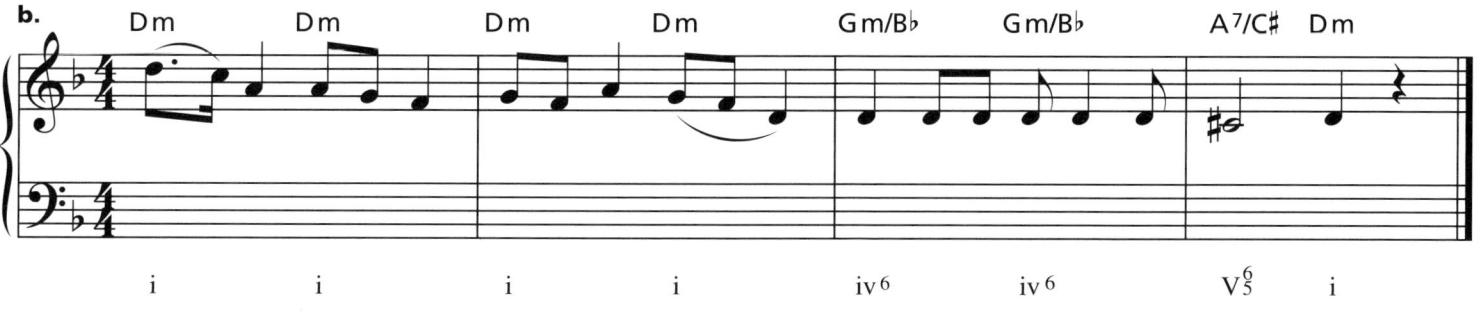

Chords: 4–32
N.H. Tones: 1.5–4.5

100

Unit 17 ACTIVITY 2 Name/Class_____

Use after completing page 109.

Composing a Melody in a Minor Key

1 Analyze the harmony provided in the following examples. Write the Roman numerals below the staff, then add the chord symbols above the staff. Write a melody and circle any non-harmonic tones, indicating whether they are passing (P), upper neighboring (U), or lower neighboring tones (L).

a.

(5th omitted)

b.
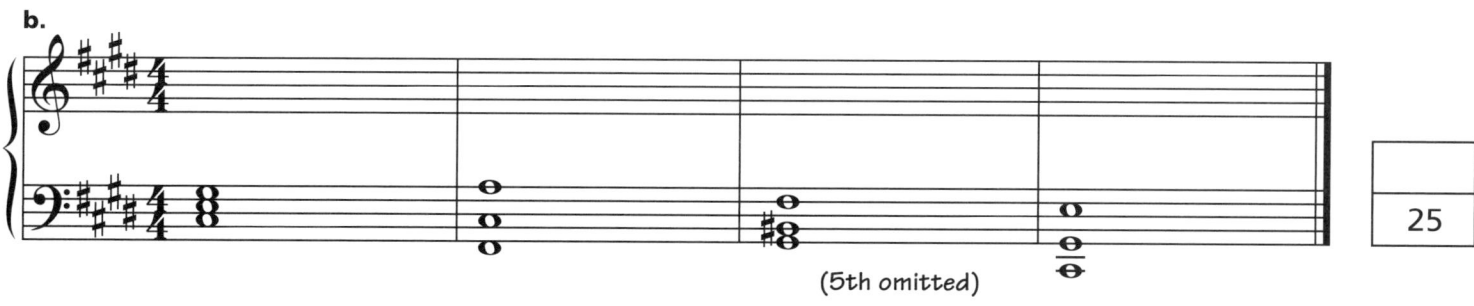
(5th omitted)

c.

(5th omitted)

d.

(5th omitted)

Copyright © MMVI by Alfred Publishing Co., Inc.

Unit 17 ACTIVITY 3 Name/Class_____

Use after completing page 110.

12-Bar Blues Chord Progression

1 A 12-bar blues chord progression has 4 measures of the _____ chord, followed by 2 measures of the _____ chord, followed by 2 measures of the _____ chord, followed by 1 measure of the V or V⁷ chord, followed by 1 measure of the _____ chord, followed by 2 measures of the I chord.

2 Write a 12-bar blues chord progression in the following keys, using the I, IV and V⁷ chords. Use inversions as needed to achieve a smooth progression between chords. Write the chord symbols above the staff and the Roman numerals below the staff for each chord, using figured bass.

a.

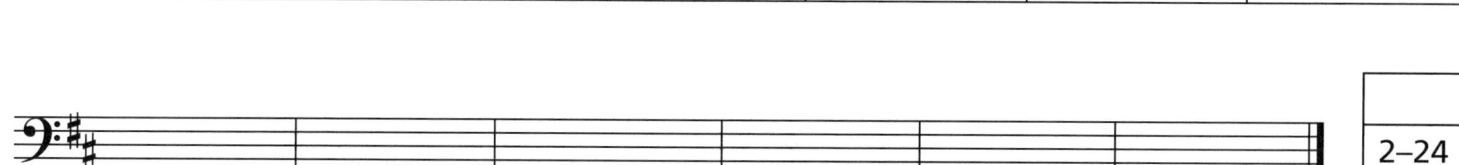

b.

c.

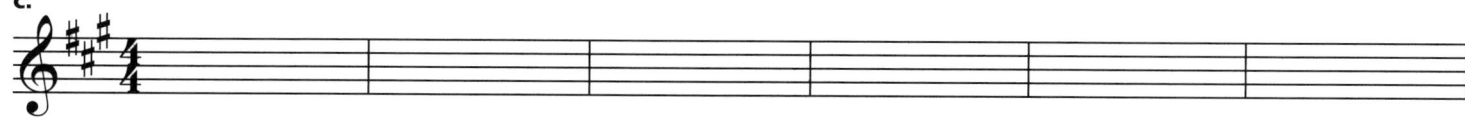

d.

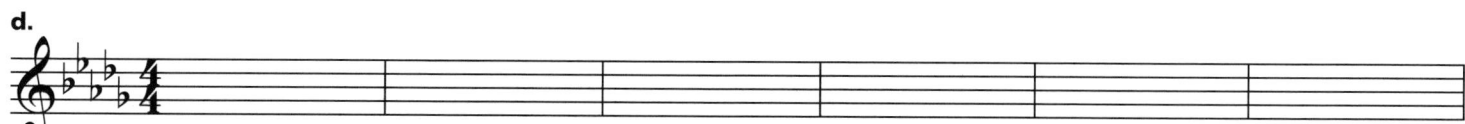

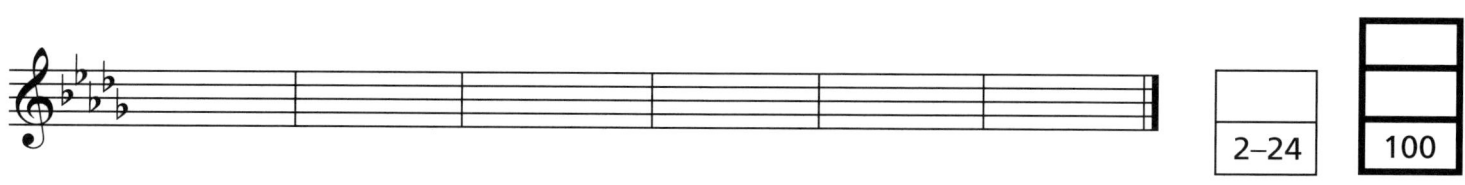

Unit 17 ACTIVITY 4 Name/Class_____

Use after completing page 111.

The Blues Scale

1 The notes of the blues scale are ____, ____, ____, ____, ____, ____, ____. 　1–7

2 Fill in the missing notes in the following blues scale. 　1–3

3 Write the blues scale in each of the following keys.

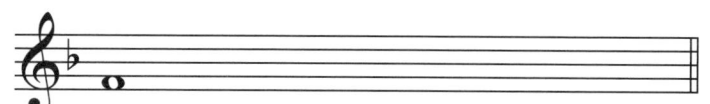 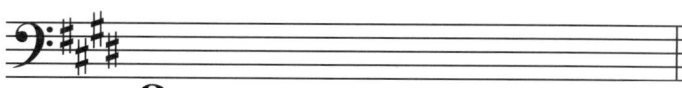

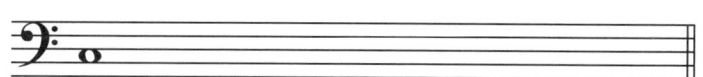 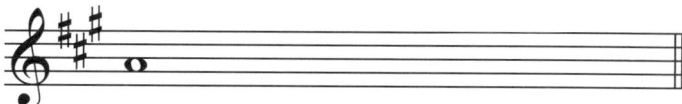

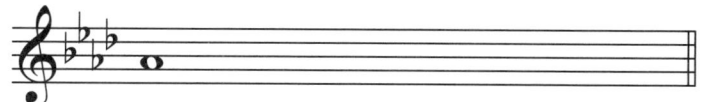 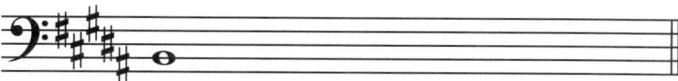

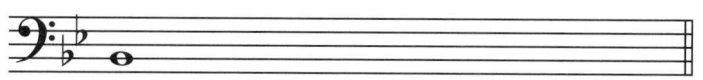 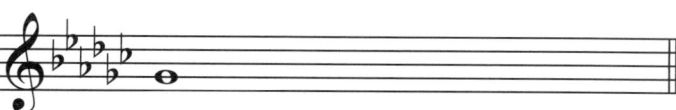

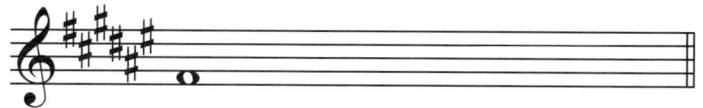

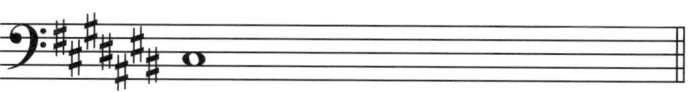 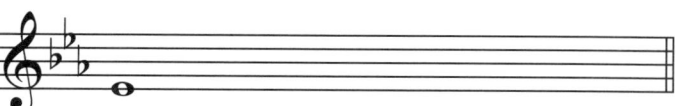

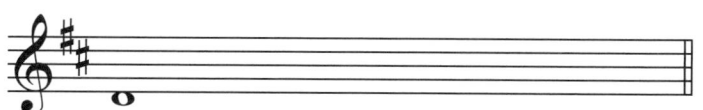 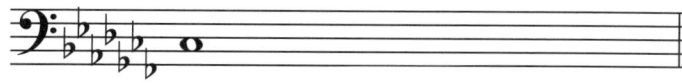

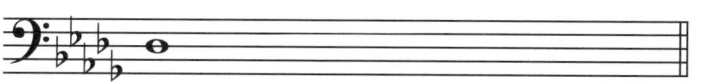 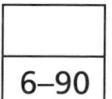　6–90

100

Copyright © MMVI by Alfred Publishing Co., Inc.

Unit 17 ACTIVITY 5 Name/Class _____

Use after completing page 111.

Composing and Harmonizing a Blues Melody

1 Write a 12-bar blues melody in a major key. Indicate the key signature and time signature at the beginning of the piece. Next, harmonize the melody using the blues chord progression. Circle the non-harmonic tones and indicate whether they are passing (P), upper neighboring (U) or lower neighboring tones (L).

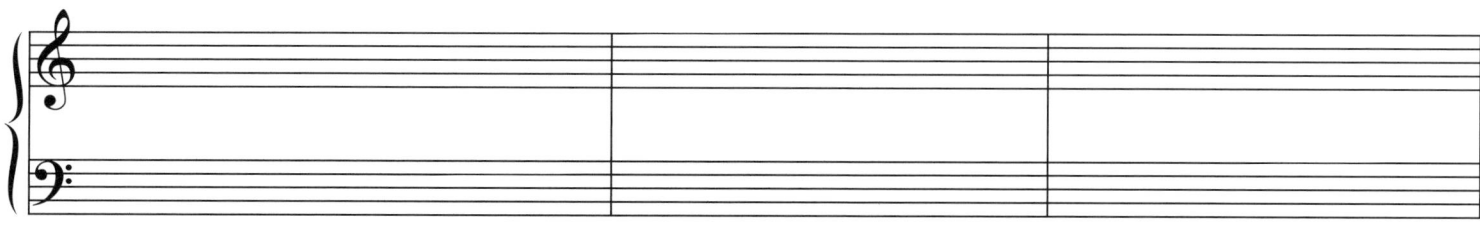

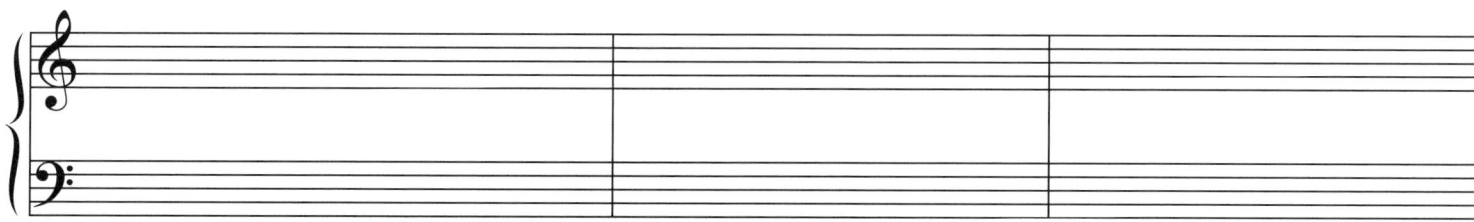

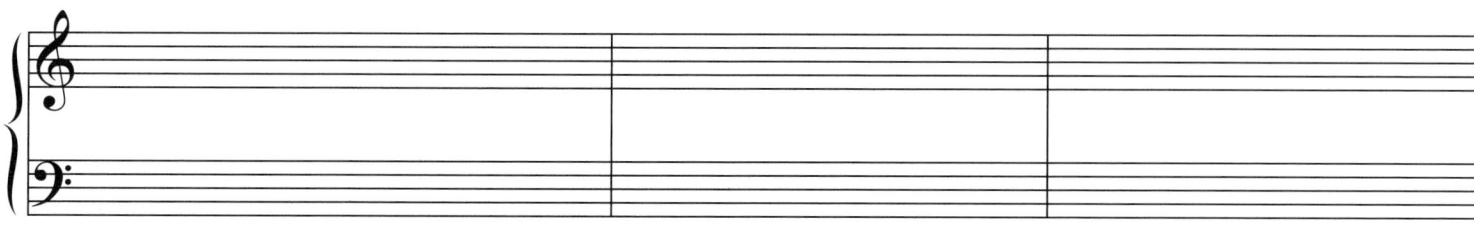

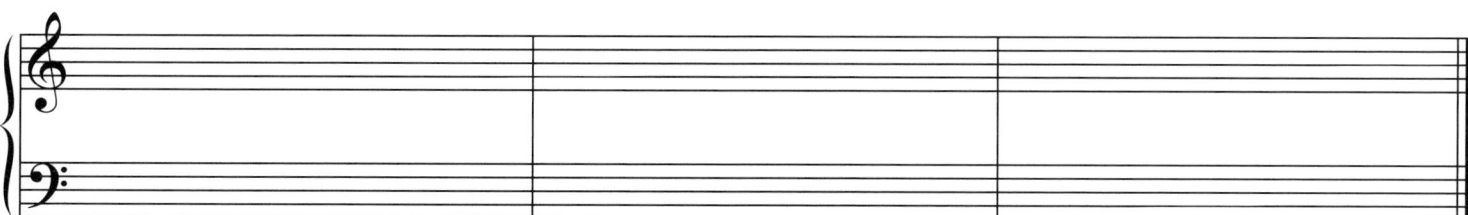

Time Sig.–3
Key Sig.–3
Melody–48
Harmony–36
N.H. Tones–10

100

Unit 17 TEST   Name/Class _____

Use after completing page 111.

1 Harmonize the following minor melody with one chord in each measure. Using i, iv and V⁷ chords only (harmonic minor scale) with inversions, write the chord symbols above the staff and the Roman numerals below the staff for each chord.

Hevenu Shalom Alechem   Israeli Folk Song

5–40

2 Analyze the harmony provided. Write the Roman numerals below the staff, then add the chord symbols above the staff. Write a melody, then circle and label any non-harmonic tones used.

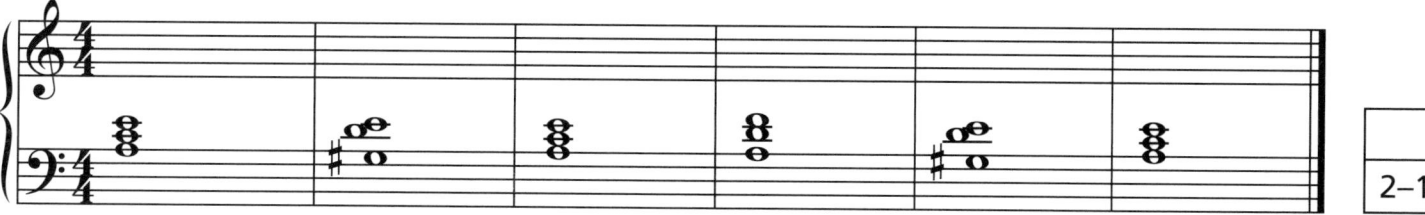

2–12

3 Write a 12-bar E♭ Blues progression in the bass staff. Write the chord symbols above the staff and the Roman numerals below the staff for each chord. Write a solo in the treble staff using the E♭ Blues scale.

Prog.–12
Solo–24
Chords–12

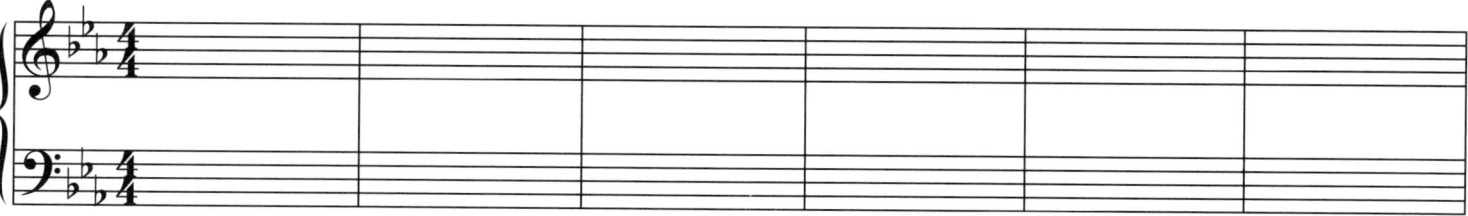

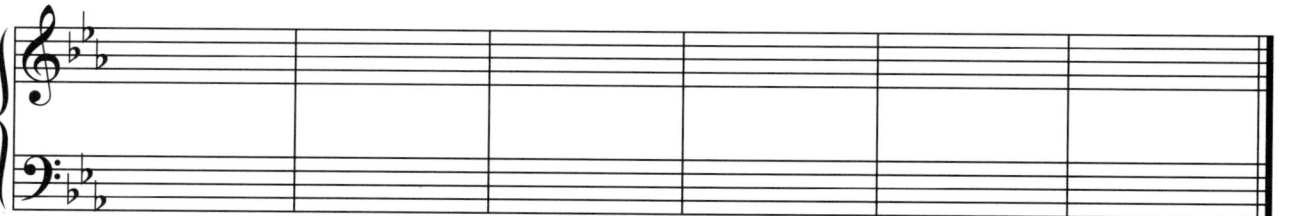

100

Copyright © MMVI by Alfred Publishing Co., Inc.

Unit 18 ACTIVITY 1 Name/Class_____

Use after completing page 114.

Basic Forms of Music–Motive and Phrase

1 Circle the motives. (Hint: Each exercise contains *either* a melodic or rhythmic motive.)

a.  4–12

b.  4–16

c.  4–12

d.  4–8

2 Circle the correct number of phrases.   1   2   3

Greensleeves

A - las, my love, you do me wrong to cast me off dis - cour - teous - ly, And
I have lov - ed you so long, De - light - ing in your com - pa - ny.

5–15

3 Circle the correct number of phrases.   1   2   3

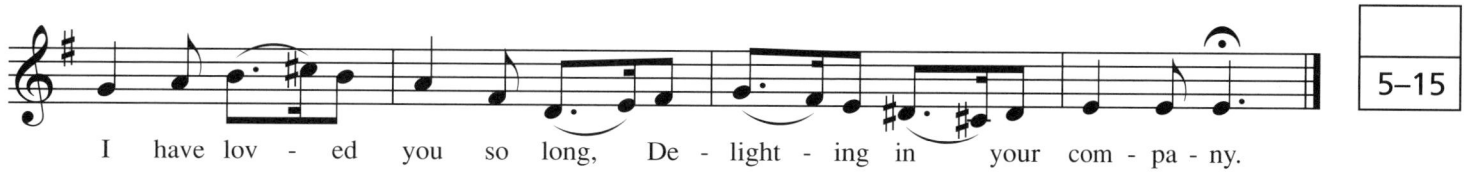

5–15

4 Circle the motives and the correct number of phrases.   1   3

Adapted from W.A. Mozart
(1756–1791)

4–16

5 Write the title of the song in exercise 3.

_____

6   100

Unit 18 **ACTIVITY 2** Name/Class_____

Use after completing page 115.

A B (Binary Form)

1 The refrain section of a song may also be called the _____.
`5`

2 List five ways that the musical elements of sections may vary from each other:
_____ _____ _____ _____ _____
`4–20`

3 Identify the following illustrations as A or AB form.

_____ _____ _____ _____ _____

`5–25`

4 Circle the correct letter of the verse in "Get on Board."   A   B

5 The refrain ends on a (circle one)
V   or   I   chord.

6 The verse ends on a (circle one)
V   or   I   chord.

7 The refrain is characterized by which type of rhythmic notes? _____

8 The verse is characterized by which type of rhythmic notes? _____

Ex. 4–8
`10–50`

Get On Board

2. The gospel train is coming, I hear it 'round the curve.
   It's using all its power, and straining every nerve!

3. The gospel train is coming, the rich and poor are there.
   No second class aboard this train, no difference in the fare!

`100`

Unit 18 **ACTIVITY 3** Name/Class_____

Use after completing page 116.

A B A (Ternary Form)

15

1 How many distinct or different sections of music are in ABA form? _____

2 Identify the following illustrations as AB or ABA form. In the final box, draw your own illustration of ABA form.

_____ _____ _____ _____ _____

5–25

3 Circle the correct letter of the verse in "Goodbye, Old Paint."   A   B

4 The refrain ends on a   V   or   I   chord. (circle one)

5 The verse is characterized by which type of rhythmic notes? _____

6 How many phrases are in the B section?   2   6

Ex. 3–6

15–60

Goodbye, Old Paint

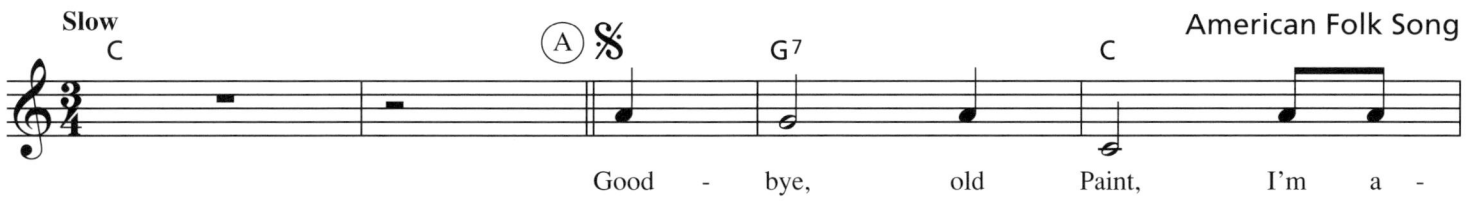

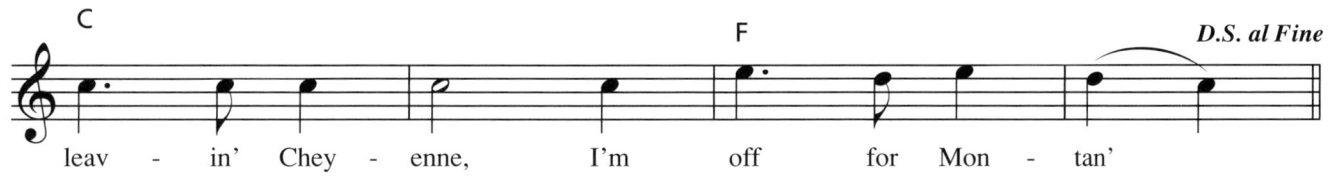

2. I'm a-ridin' old Paint, I'm a-leadin' old Fan. Good-by, little Annie, I'm off for Cheyenne.

3. Oh, hitch up your horses, And feed them some hay, And seat yourself by me, As long as you stay.

100

Copyright © MMVI by Alfred Publishing Co., Inc.   35

Unit 18 **ACTIVITY 4** Name/Class_____

Use after completing page 117.

Rondo Form

1 In rondo form, the _____ section alternates with other contrasting sections.

[11]

2 Circle the rondo forms: ABACA   ABBC   ABCD   ABACABA

[6–12]

3 Arrange the following [A form] folk songs into an ABACADA rondo by writing their titles in correct order: "Get On Board;" "She'll Be Coming 'Round the Mountain;" "Row, Row, Row Your Boat;" "Down By the Station."

_____

_____

_____

_____

_____

[5–35]

4 Write the Roman numerals below the staff (one chord per measure), fill in the section letter at the beginning of each stave in the circle provided, then circle the form:

[2–42]

Bodhi Rondo   ABACABA   ABACA   ABABA

George Field

[100]

Copyright © MMVI by Alfred Publishing Co., Inc.

Unit 18 **ACTIVITY 5** Name/Class_____

Use after completing page 117.

Form Review

1 A motive may be identified by any of the following musical characteristics:

_____ , _____ or _____ .

7–21

2 The following example contains a rhythmic and a melodic motive. Circle each example of the rhythmic motive, and draw a box around each example of the melodic motive.

Symphony No. 8 in B minor, "Unfinished"   Franz Schubert (1797–1828)

7–49

3 Identify the number of phrases in the example from "Vaga luna, che inargenti."   2   3   4

Vaga luna, che inargenti   Vincenzo Bellini (1801–1835)

15

4 Circle the form of "Minuet."   A   AB   ABA   ABACA

Minuet (from the Notebook for Anna Magdalena Bach)   Johann Sebastian Bach (1685–1750)

15   100

Copyright © MMVI by Alfred Publishing Co., Inc.   37

Unit 18 **TEST** Name/Class_____

Use after completing page 117.

1 A short section of music that expresses a complete or incomplete musical idea is called a _____.   20

2 A small melodic, rhythmic or harmonic element used repeatedly throughout a piece is called a _____.   20

3 Write an example of Rondo form using letters: _____   20

4 Circle the number of phrases.   2   3   5

Aria (from the Notebook for Anna Magdalena Bach)   Johann Sebastian Bach (1685–1750)

So oft ich mei - ne To - backs Pfei - fe, mit gu - tem Kna - ster an - ge - füllt,

5 Circle the form of *The Wild Rider*.   20

A   AB   ABA   ABACADA   ABACA

The Wild Rider   Robert Schumann (1810–1856)

20 | 100

Copyright © MMVI by Alfred Publishing Co., Inc.

Answer Keys

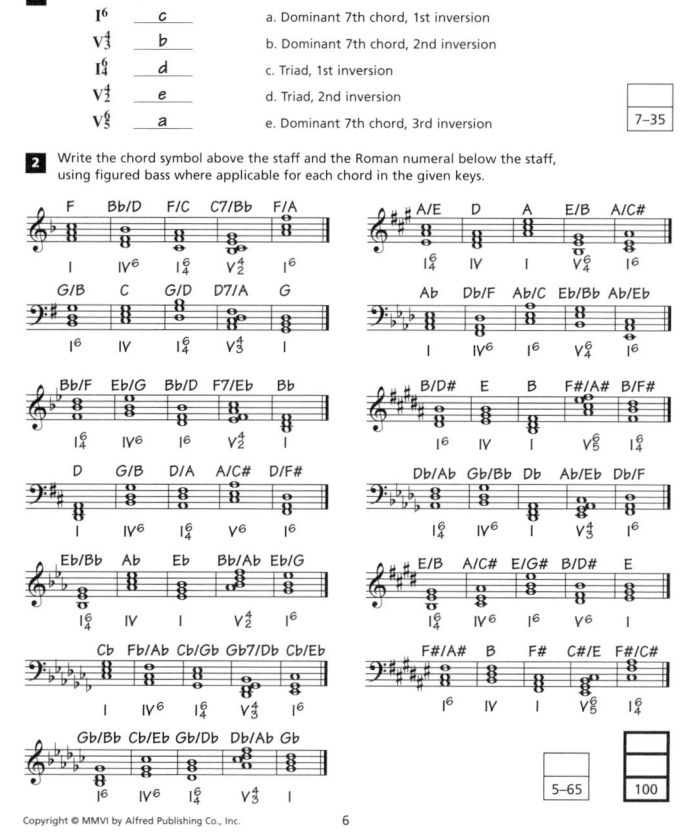

39

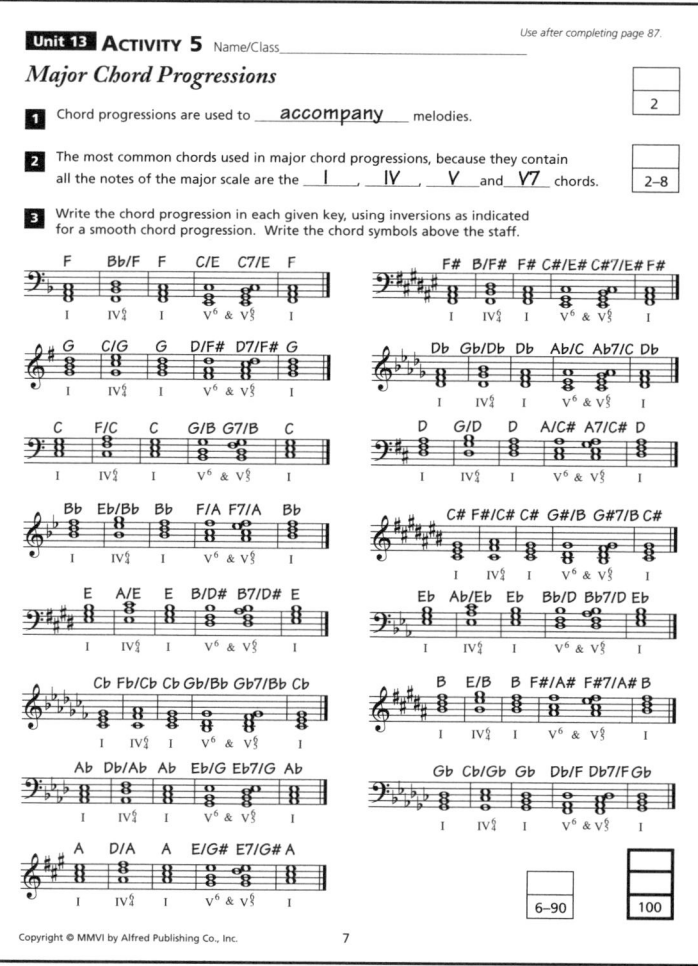
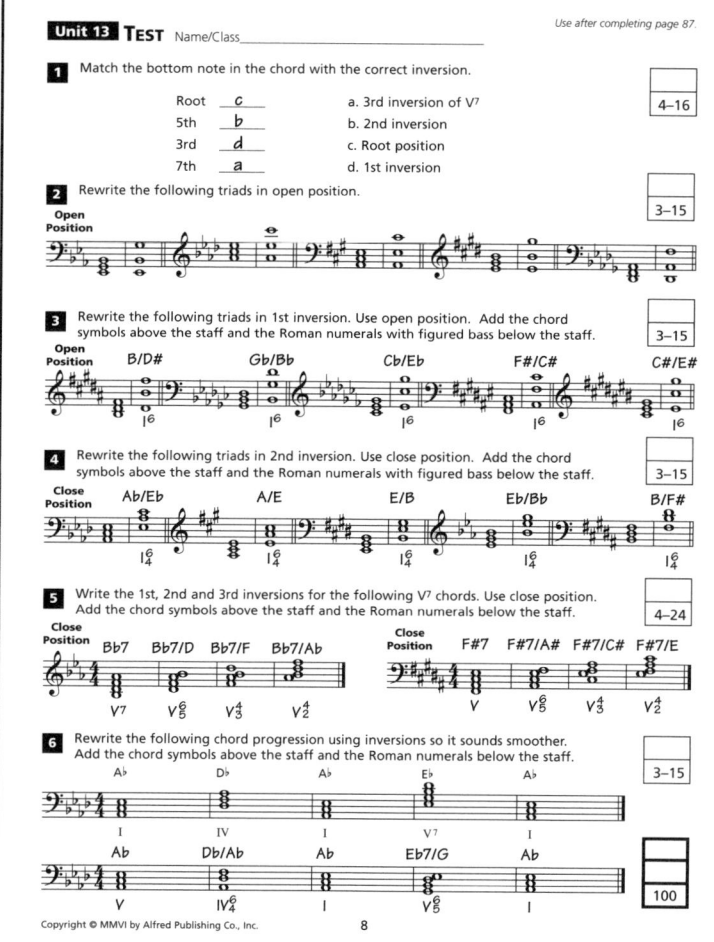
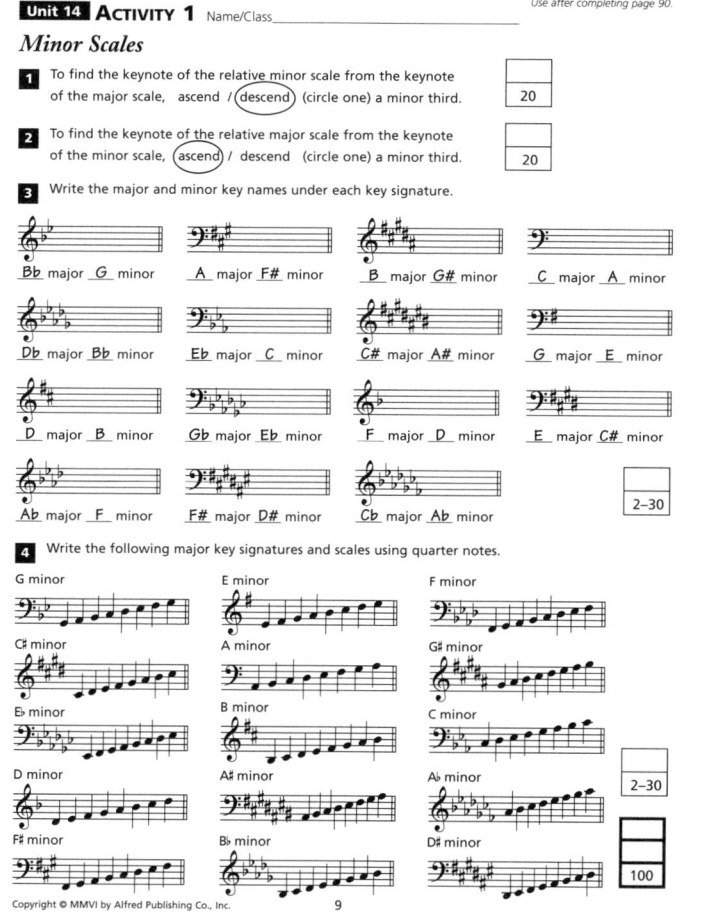
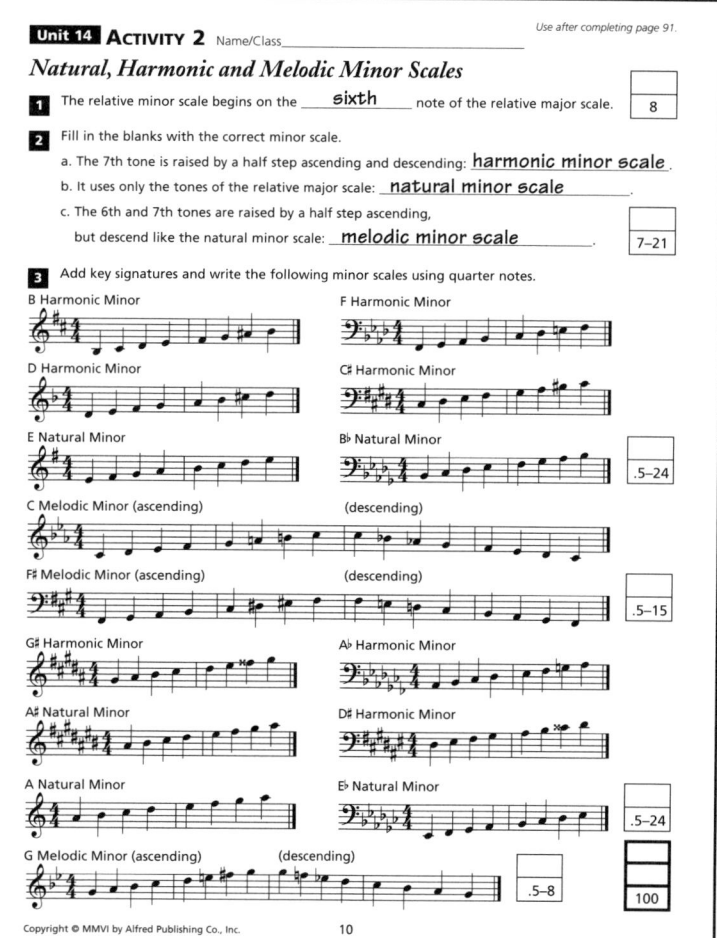

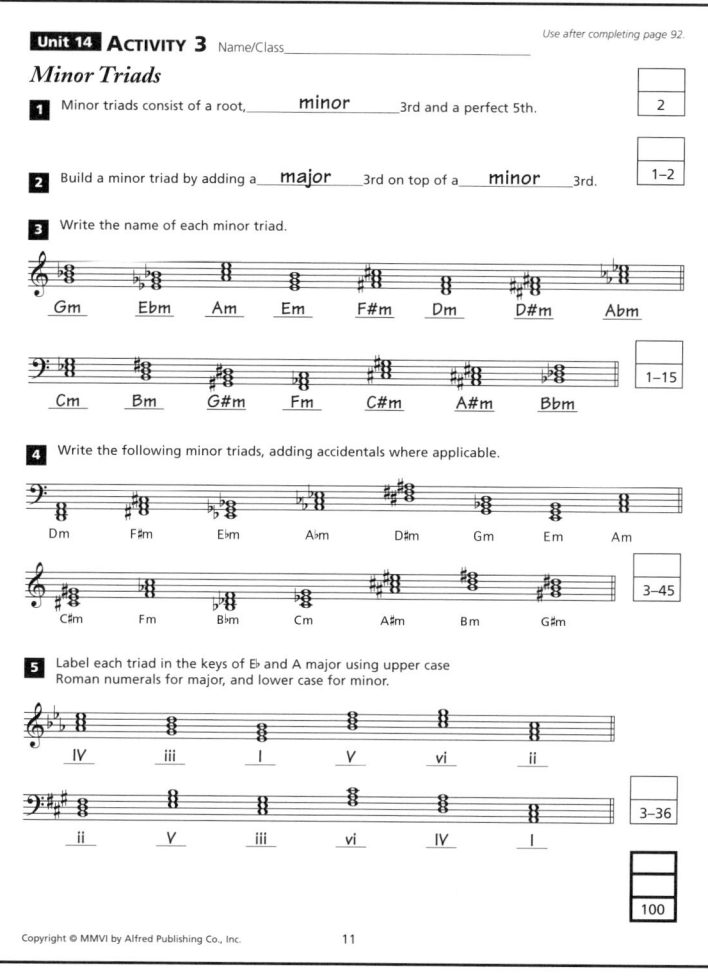
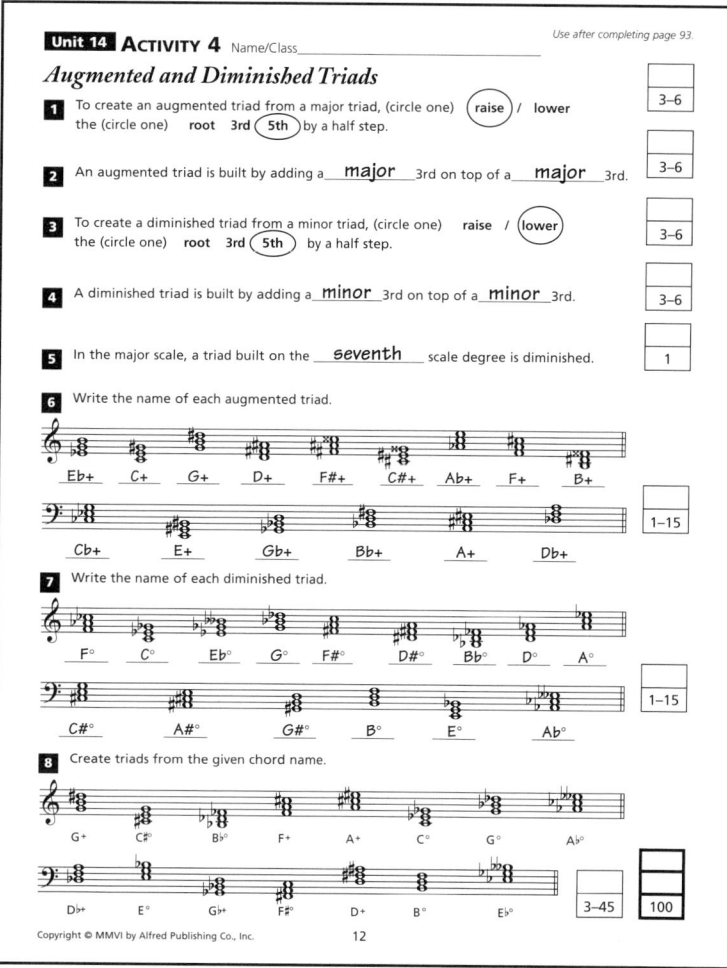
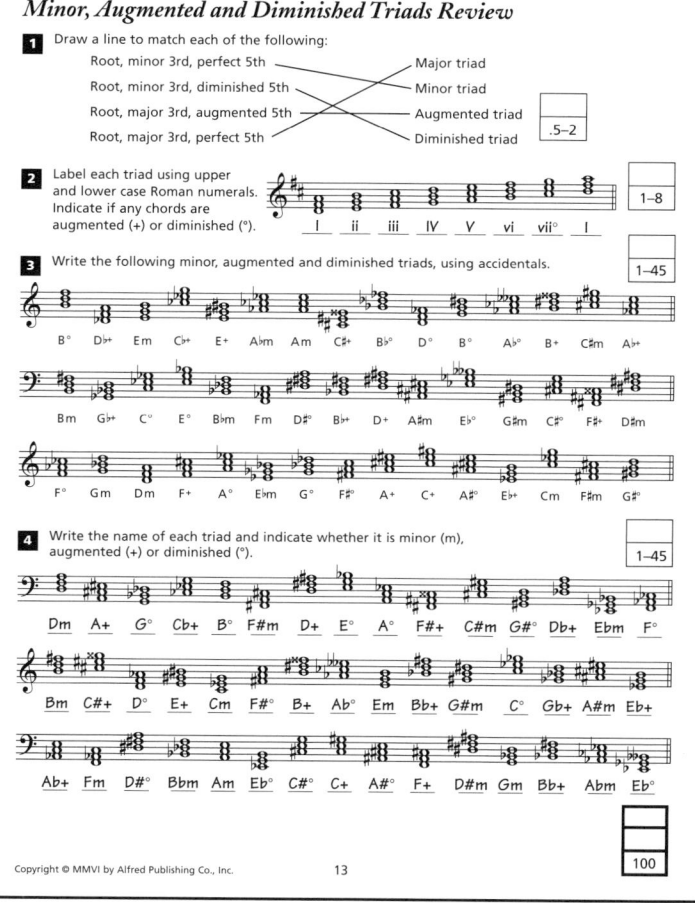
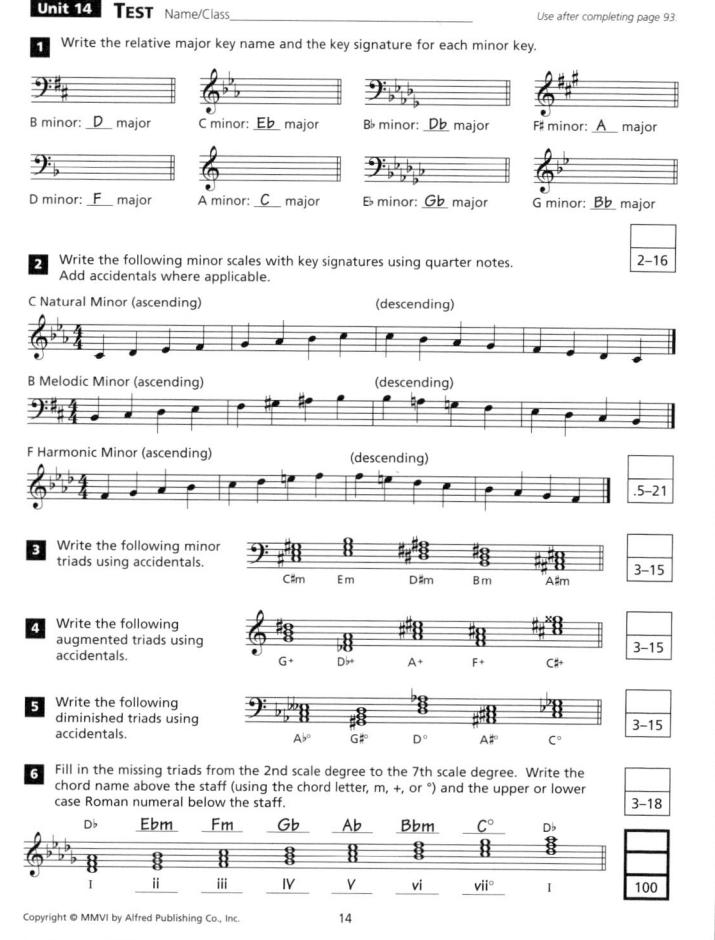

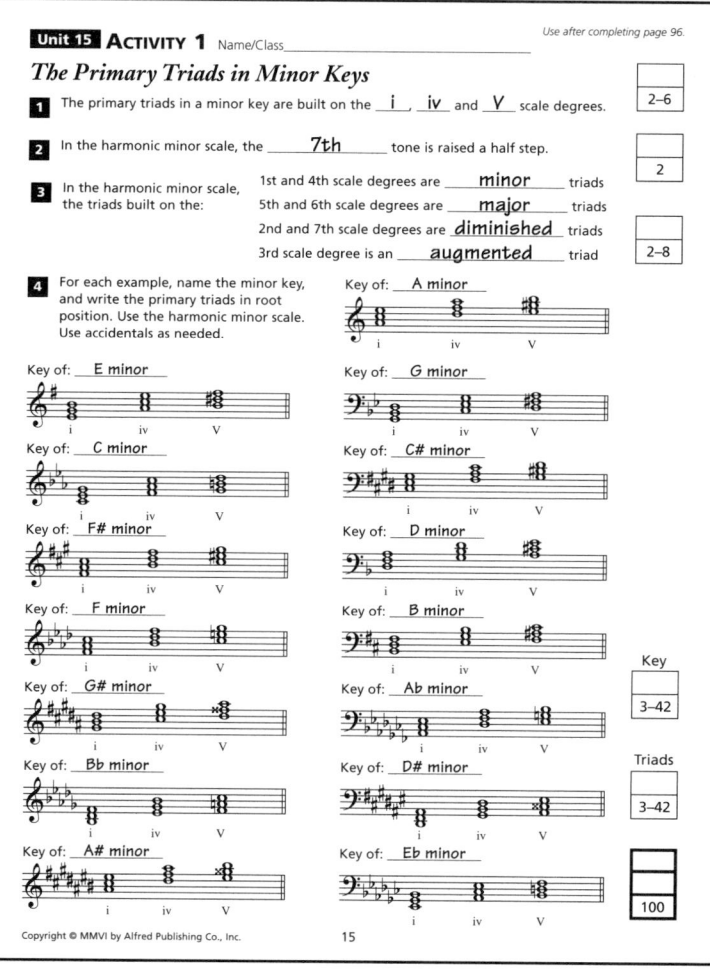
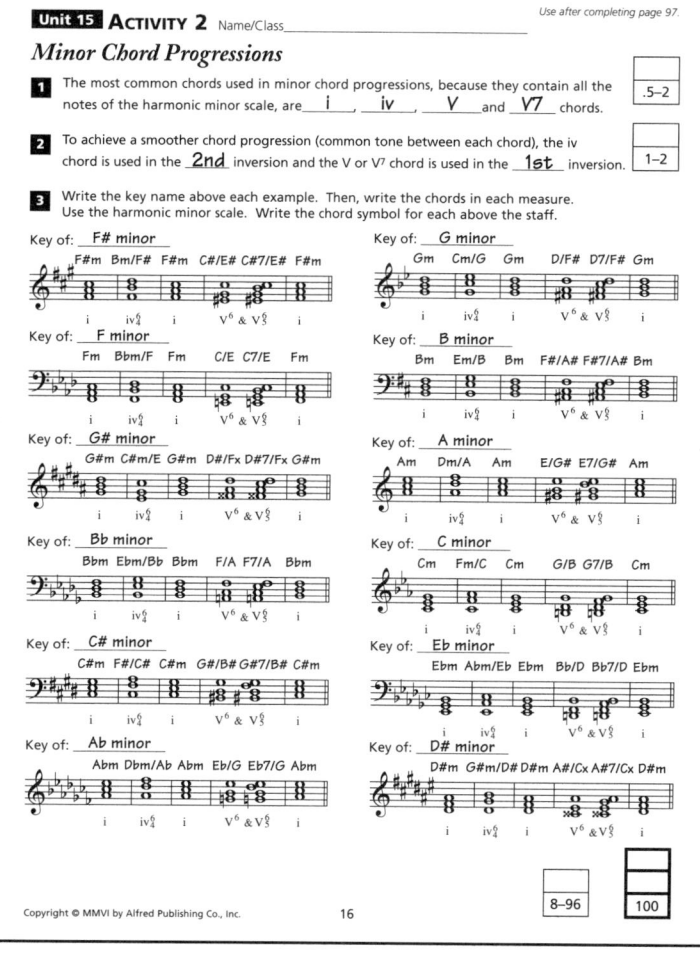
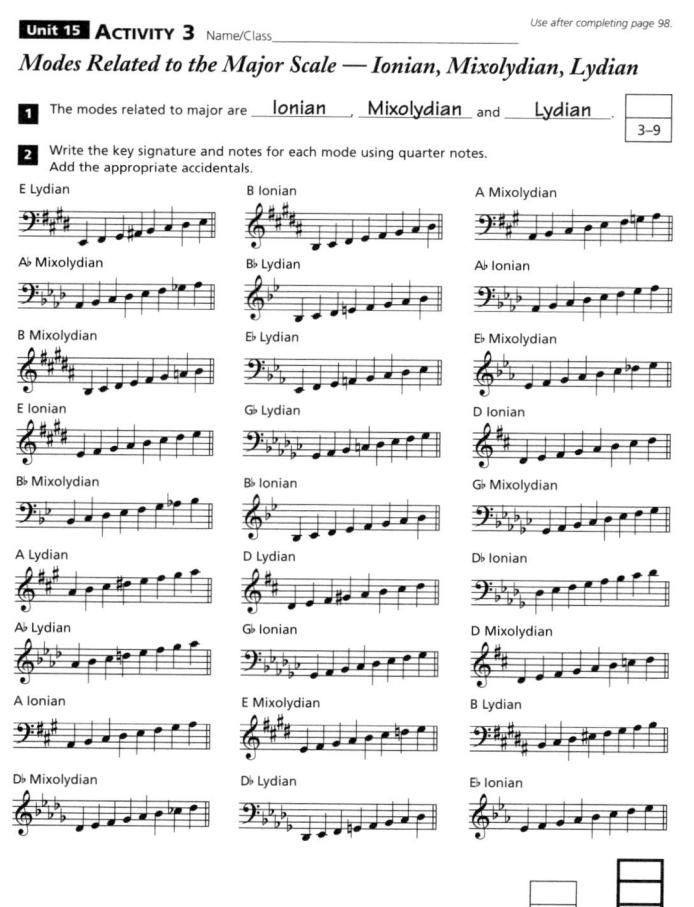
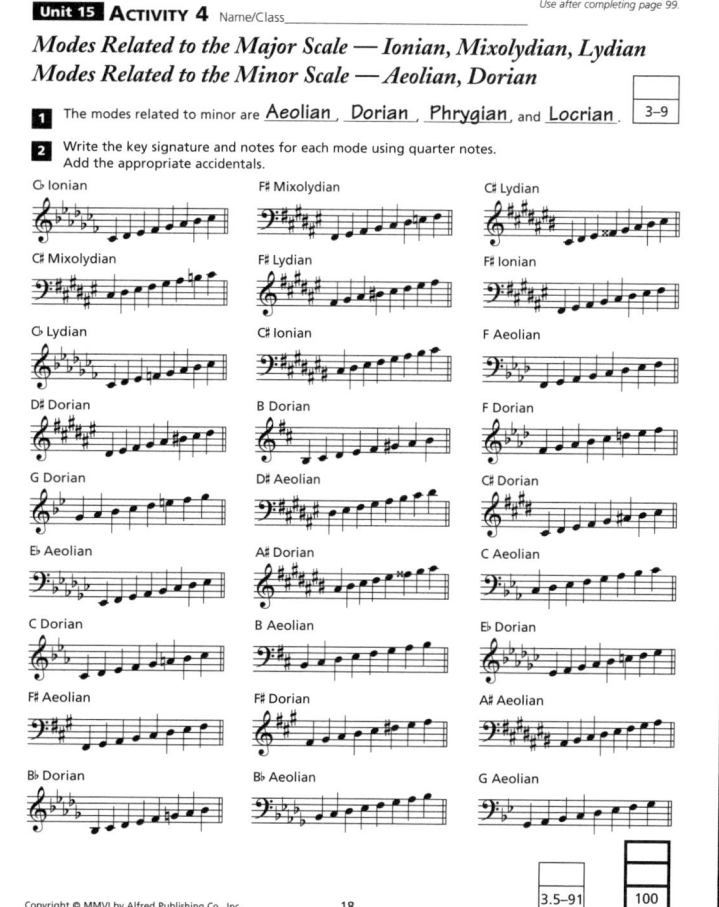

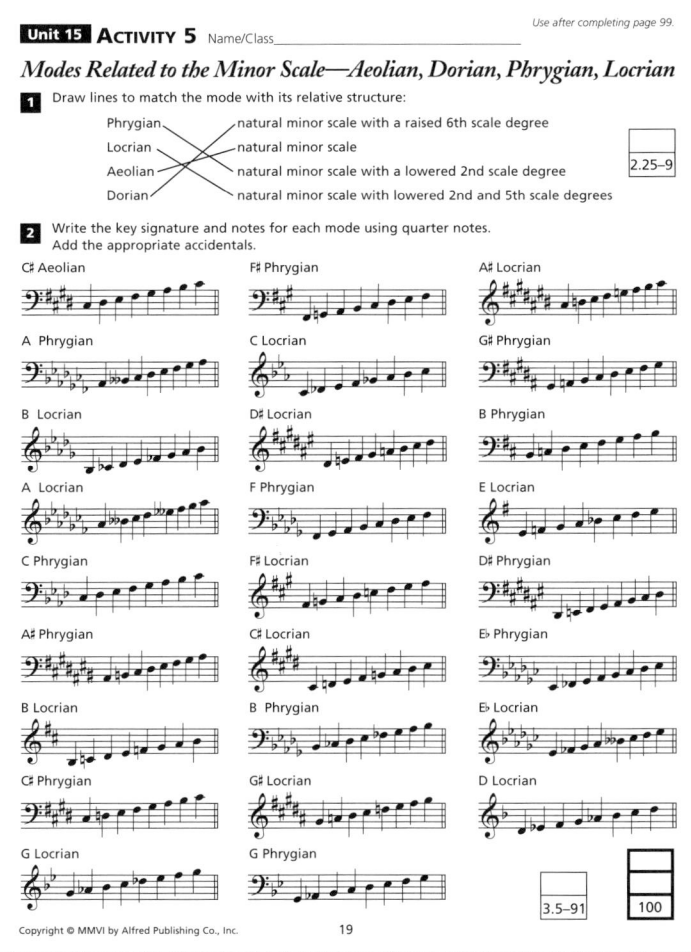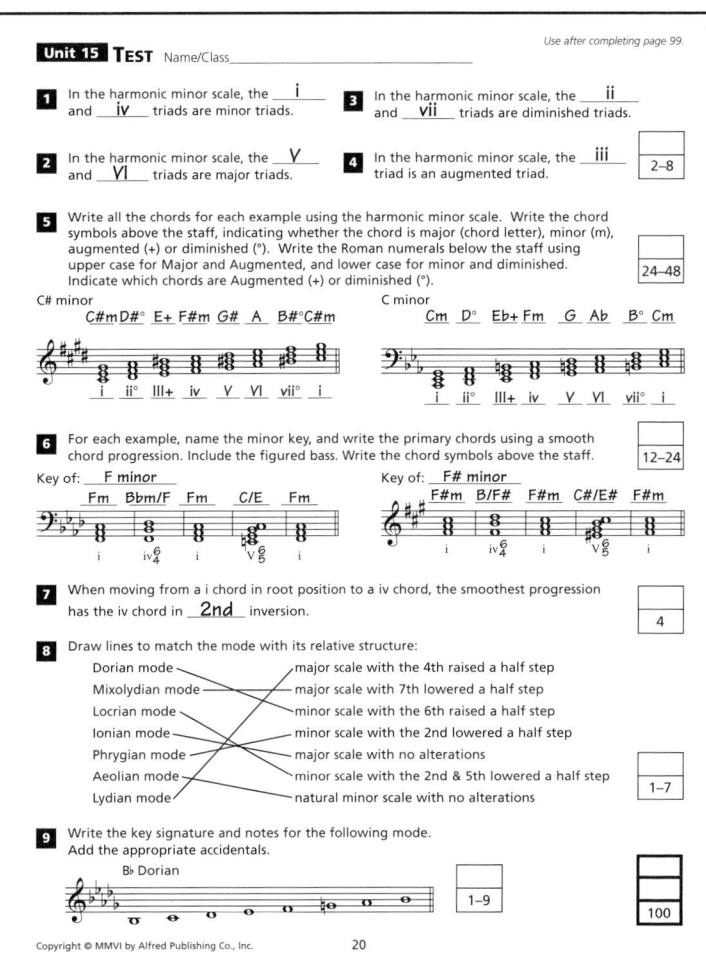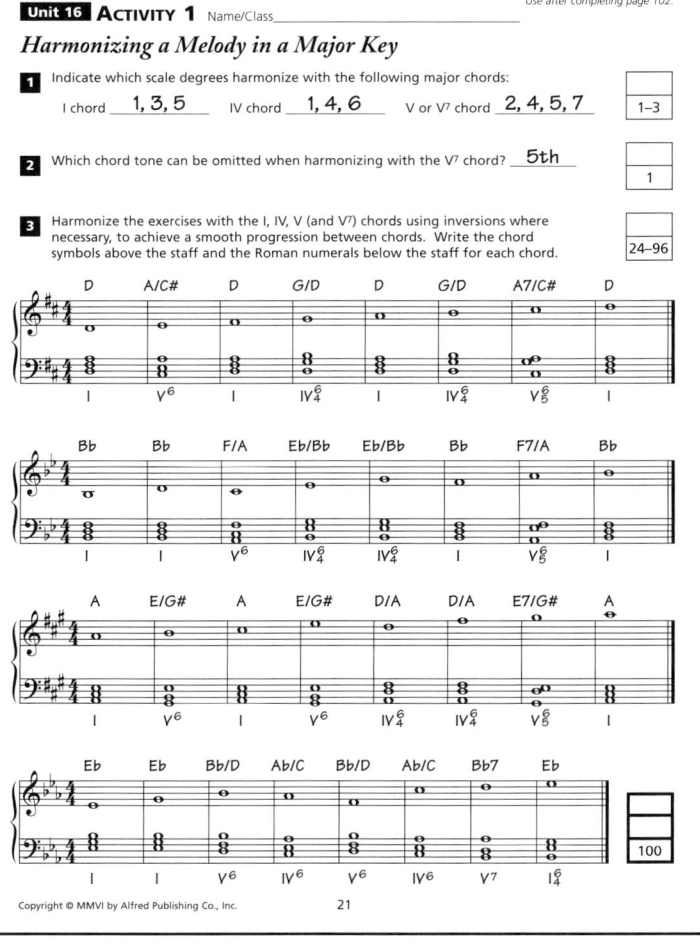

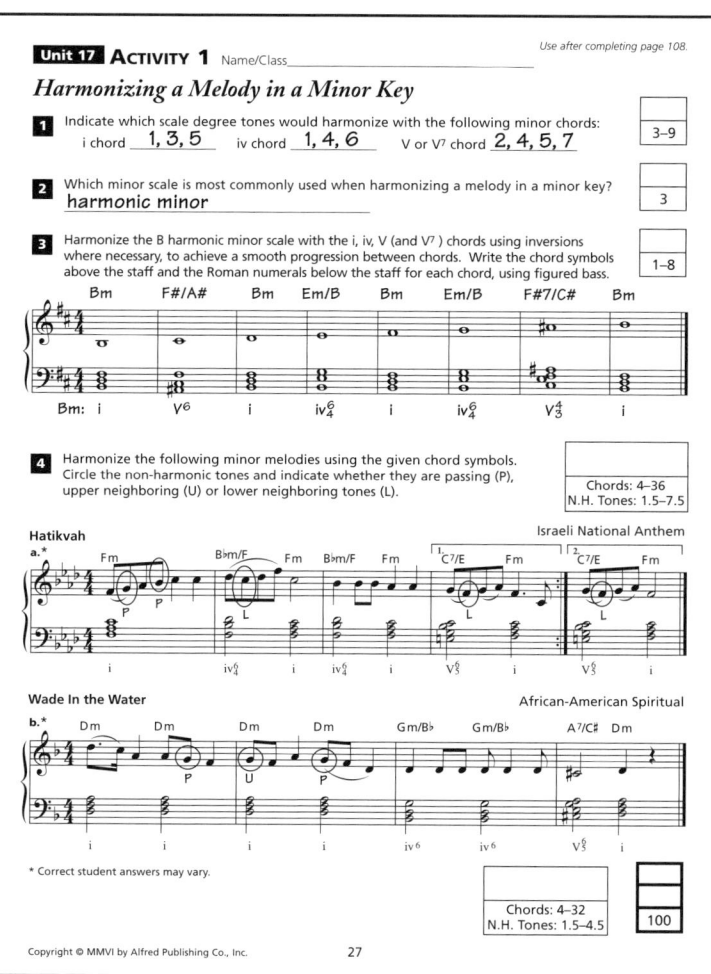
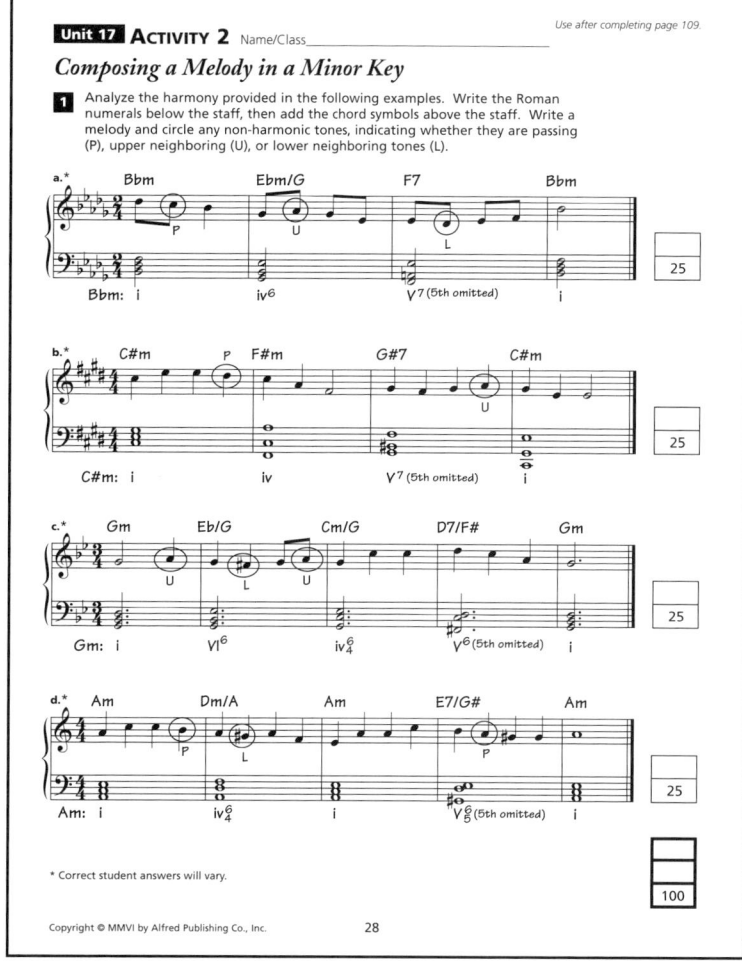
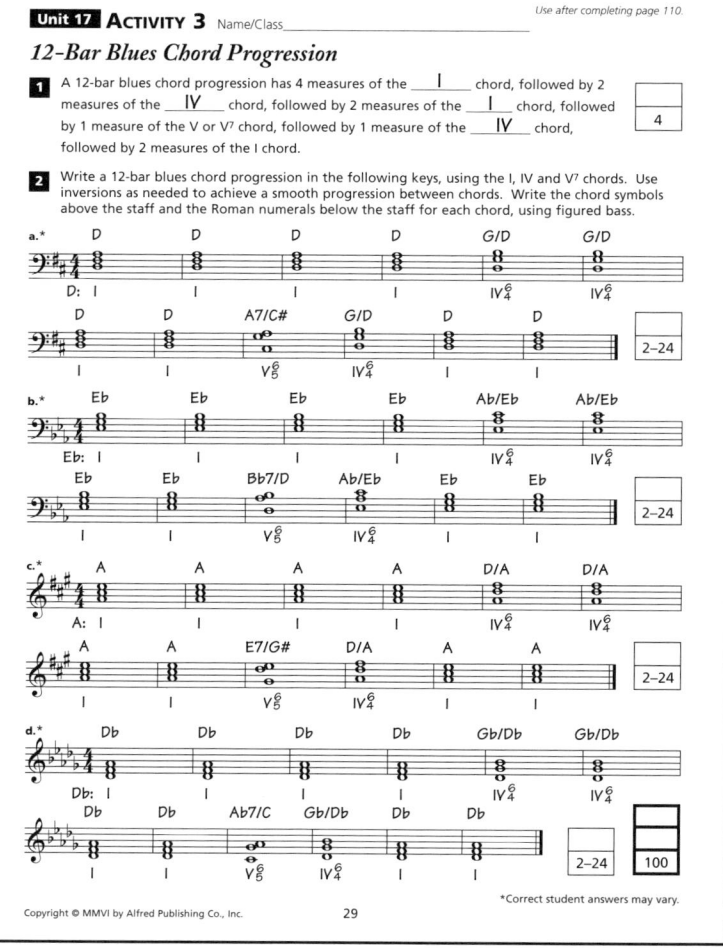
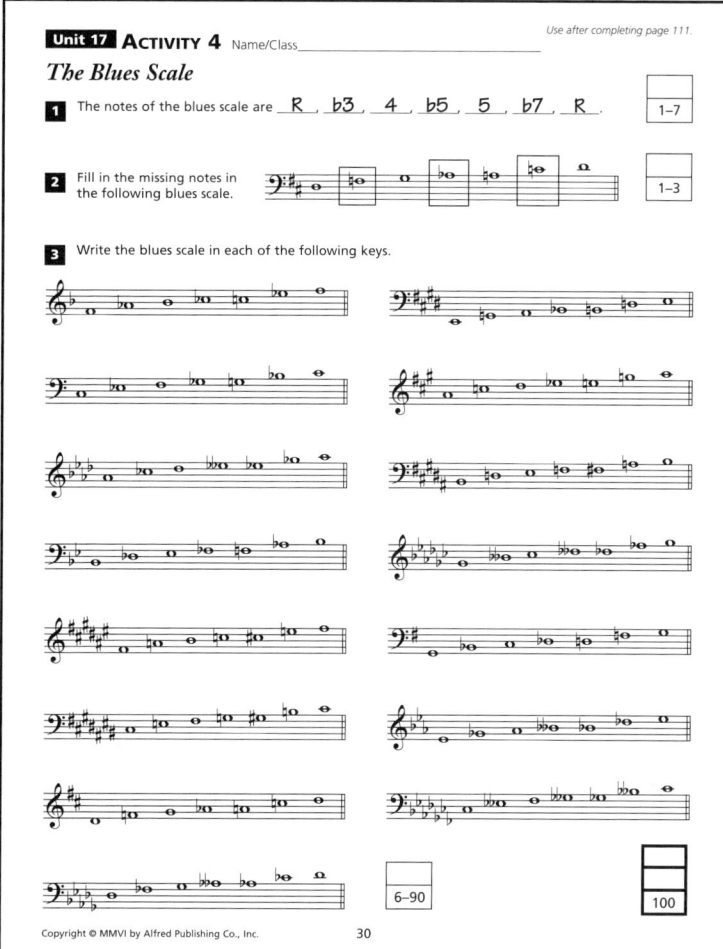

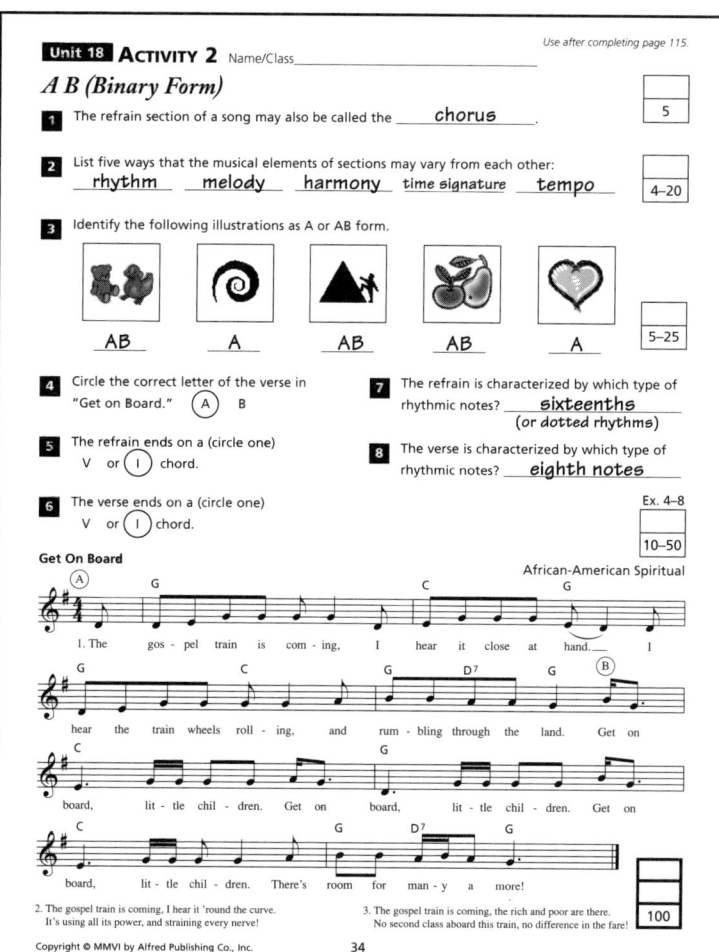

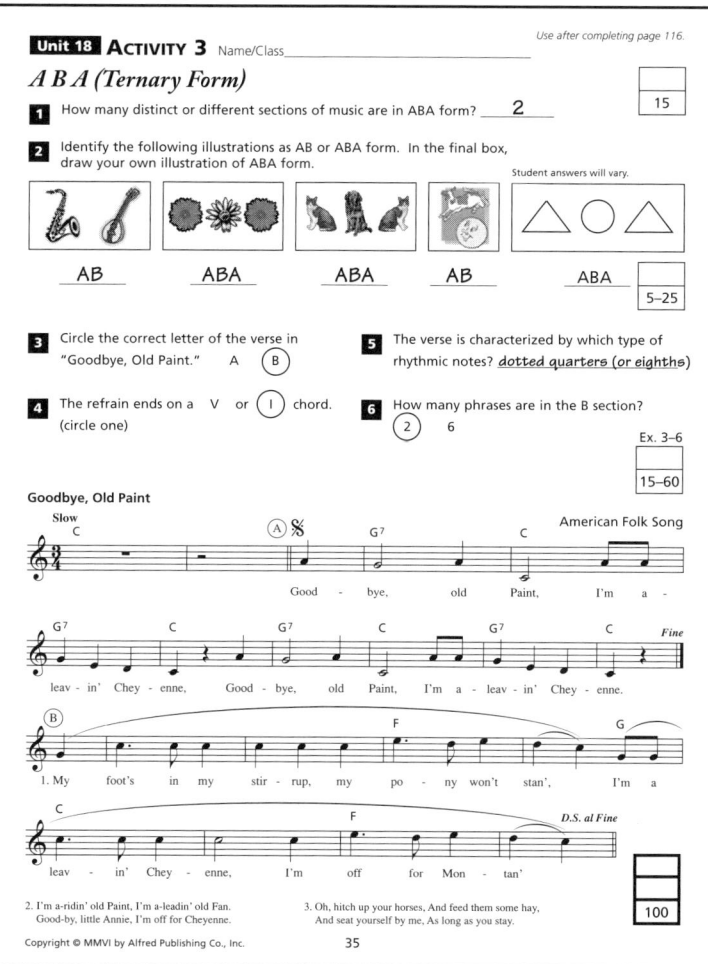
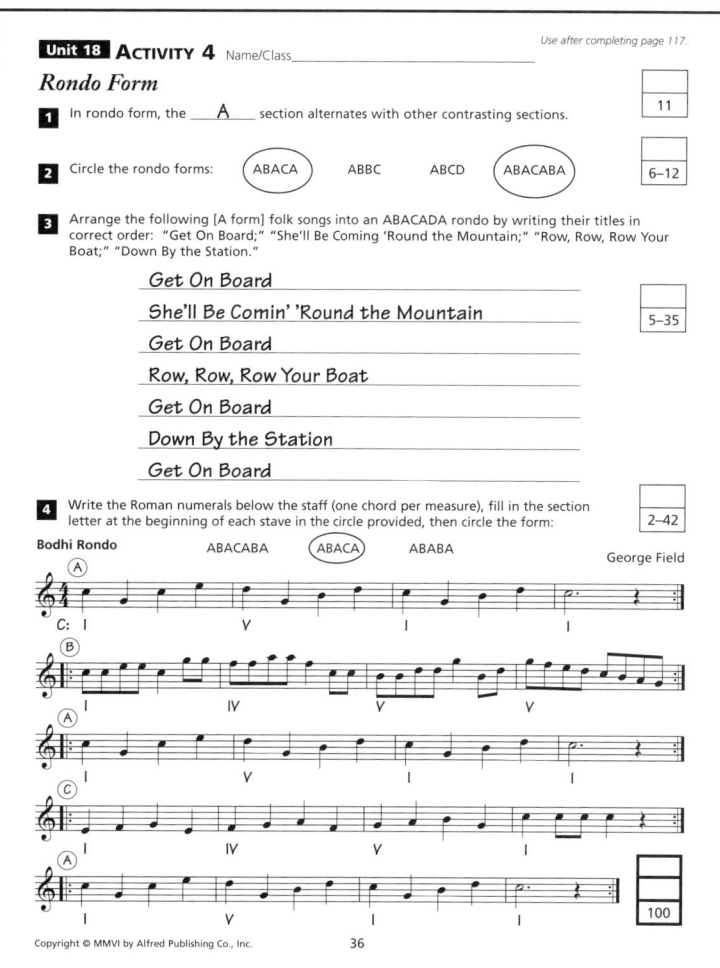

Grade Form for Activities and Tests in Alfred's Essentials of Music Theory Teacher's Activity Kit

School Term _____ Class _____

Student Name	Book 3							Unit ___							Unit ___							Unit ___						
	1	2	3	4	5	T		1	2	3	4	5	T		1	2	3	4	5	T		1	2	3	4	5	T	